T0159144

Portal to Darkness

The Maya Lords of the Underworld Awakened

Michael "Chip" Coronel

authorHOUSE®

AuthorHouse™
1663 Liberty Drive
Bloomington, IN 47403
www.authorhouse.com
Phone: 1 (800) 839-8640

Published by AuthorHouse 04/02/2018

ISBN: 978-1-5462-3495-1 (sc)
ISBN: 978-1-5462-3493-7 (hc)
ISBN: 978-1-5462-3494-4 (e)

Library of Congress Control Number: 2018903642

Print information available on the last page.

Any people depicted in stock imagery provided by Getty Images are models, and such images are being used for illustrative purposes only. Certain stock imagery © *Getty Images.*

This book is printed on acid-free paper.

Cover Design and Illustration: Zach Britton

CONTENTS

Chapter 1 1
Chapter 2 6
Chapter 3 14
Chapter 4 19
Chapter 5 22
Chapter 6 26
Chapter 7 30
Chapter 8 37
Chapter 9 40
Chapter 10 43
Chapter 11 48
Chapter 12 50
Chapter 13 52
Chapter 14 60
Chapter 15 63
Chapter 16 74
Chapter 17 98

Epilogue 105

For my forever wife and best friend since the day I met her.

I would like to thank my colleagues and friends for their support, contributions and insights. Dr. Patricia Crane Coronel, Colorado State University, Dr. Catherine DiCesare, Colorado State University, Dr. Tomas Santos, University of Northern Colorado and Joel Long for his editing and suggestions.

Maya Glyph for Xibalba, The Maya Underworld

CHAPTER 1

Rosalia Canul was returning to Palenque, Guatemala for the first time since she left for college to study her own Mayan culture. She was going to meet up in Palenque with a Mayan scholar, Anthony Michael, who she hadn't met in person though his writings were familiar to her as they related to her own research. The trip was going to be long, including a plane flight from Texas, but the most arduous aspect would be the famed Guatemalan buses, single lane dirt roads, winding through thick jungles, piloted by fearless drivers that applied their brakes sparingly.

Now on her way, there was plenty of time to remember Mayan experiences from the past and reorganize her research notes for this upcoming study with Anthony.

She thought of many myths and legends about ancient Maya, but her specific academic interests with deciphering the meanings of glyphs that marked the ruins of temples and tombs were those she wanted to relate to myths. Those were the ones her uncle, Miguel, told her when she was young. He related stories about 19th century explorers led by their Mayan guides first discovered the ruins. As a child he seemed like the most knowledgeable person in her universe when he told her these historical adventures. She thought now that her fascination with his stories, especially the myth of the hero twins who descended underground to the land where the Mayan Lords lived and ruled, were a guiding force that lead her to her own academic studies and the subject of her dissertation. Since Miguel worked as a guide and interpreter with scholars, he had first-hand accounts of explorations.

She was returning to Palenque with a new understanding, interest and more Mayan knowledge. Her uncle's expedition stories were reinforced as historically accurate when she heard her professors elaborate on what she remembered as bedtime stories told by her uncle. The most frightening one was about the 19th century explorers, Lloyd Stephens an American adventurist and Frederick Catherwood, an English architect and artist, who discovered or rediscovered the ancient city of Copan in 1840.

Rosalia could hear uncle's voice. The explorers had trekked for days and in high temperatures and humidity through difficult terrain in the Honduran jungle. This expedition had been far more exhausting than anything they had ever experienced. She could only imagine their sweat and fatigue and as they were rewarded along the way with glimpses of what seemed to them the most magnificent Mayan ruins imaginable, revealed only momentarily through the dense jungle growth. Each moss covered stone seemed to beg to be acknowledged. Roasalia could only wish to have experienced their excitement, rather than taking the local bus to the ruins.

Stephens' earlier expeditions included an exploration of the holy lands, followed with a published journal of the same name. One chapter of his journal was dedicated to Egypt and what he later referred to as the "Moses connection." He had become fascinated with all things Egyptian and particularly the pyramids at Giza. As an American he was a relatively late to Egyptology studies. Numerous English explorers and archeologists had already begun the essential exploration and systematic study of Egypt, so he felt more like a tourist on a 19th century European "Grand Tour." His Egyptology goals changed totally by chance or fate because of a casual conversation with an archeology student assisting on a dig at the great Stepped Pyramid at Saqqara. She was a young artist hired to draw and paint faithful renditions of the sites. After days of conversation on recent archeological studies, she directly asked him, "What are you doing in Egypt? Why aren't you in Mexico." "That's where my professor says all the real discoveries are happening." Stephens was shocked! He asked what she meant since to him Egypt was the "Holy Grail" of Archeology.

She began to describe what her professor had told her that Egypt had already been "discovered!" He simply said all the major sites have been explored/excavated. She had read recent accounts on amazing new discoveries were occurring in Mexico.

With that comment intuition guided Stephens to take the next boat to America. Shortly after his arrival in the United States, he fortunately met up with an English architect and artist, Fredrick Catherwood, whom he knew shared his interests in exploration. Catherwood was encouraged by Stephens' enthusiasm.

They were soon on a journey quest for the ancient Mayan city of Copan. Stephens, who was the more experienced of the two, thought that their guides had found the destination when they arrived at a monumental architectural site, now overgrown with years of jungle vegetation. Vines covered the entrances of all the temples, evidence that no one had entered them in centuries. For Stephens, it felt like a jewel in the rough; he had discovered a time capsule. He had no idea how soon all that would change.

On the third night several of the native porters and their guide, Arturo, who was the only one who understood English and their fragmented Spanish, came over to their campfire to tell them that the porters were amused by their interest in the temples and Catherwood's drawings. The oldest porter spoke for some time to the Mexican guide in his native Mayan dialect. The guide only nodded and occasionally made hand gestures pointing toward the south. Finally the porter stopped, and smiling with an enormous grin he winked at Stephens.

The guide began, "He is only a laborer but he says he knows of a city that is much grander than this, with many temples and a tower unlike anything he has ever seen. Only his people, the Quiche know where it is located."

Stephens went to his backpack and pulled out a book with a beautiful leather cover in a deep red patina. It was his prized possession, a rare copy of *Constituciones diocesanas del obispado de Chiappa* written in 1702 by Francisco Nunez de la Vega, Bishop of Chiapa. He had purchased it in Mexico City in small bookstore for only a few pesos. The owner was trying to sell the book more for its leather cover than the contents. Stephens used the silk ribbon bookmark to immediately turn to the section it marked. He began reading Nunez's account of a city he had journeyed to that was unlike any of the other Mayan cites. Compared to most of his observations that were notably negative concerning the pagan natives and their cultural and religious peculiarities, this city seemed to hold an almost magical nostalgia. What frustrated Stephens was that Nunez, for some unknown reason, failed to name the city. This was peculiar since he been meticulous in recording all the sites that he had visited, listing both the Mayan and Spanish names. He asked the porter if this was the city. The porter smiled and nodded. The next morning they broke camp.

After three weeks of impenetrable jungle, on the afternoon of January 28, 1840 John Lloyd Stephens and Frederick Catherwood saw their first glimpse of the ruins of the lost Mayan city of Palenque. It was magical. The torrential rain was now only an intermittent sprinkle, and they could see a low-lying valley veiled in fog. Stephens was the first to see it at the far end was the tower. He felt something touching his hand. He looked down and there was Arturo with his face beaming, saying "Si, Si, Si!" Stephens could only nod and smile back, "Si."

They set up camp in the ruins of the large sprawling structure adjacent to the tower. It had an open courtyard, surrounded on three sides by a series of rooms. They named it 'The Palace' since Catherwood remarked it had to be since it was so grand. Later archeologists would validate his assumption.

In the morning they began exploring the site. The most prominent structure besides the tower and palace complex was a magnificent temple. It was raised on nine enormous tiered levels, culminating in a three-roomed structure on the top. The interior was filled with debris, partially collapsed stucco and the once beamed ceiling was now covered with heavy jungle overgrowth. They spent several hours attempting to clear an entrance to the first chamber. When the sun was beginning to set, the guide suggested that it would be better to begin again in the morning. Stephens and Catherwood reluctantly agreed.

This began as a routine night. Their guide and the porters prepared the dinner comprised of the all too familiar rice and beans then Catherwood and Stephens sat by the campfire drinking sparingly from their next to last bottle of gin. After dinner they each retired to their respective tents, the guide and porters still not understanding why they preferred to 'camp out' when they could sleep in the palace rooms.

At some unknown hour of the night, Stephens was awakened from his sleep by a strange vibrating sound, pulsating like an enormous heart beat. Then he heard the porters shouting to Arturo something that he could only make out occasional words spoken in Spanish. They were pointing at the temple.

Catherwood, sound asleep, awoke startled when he heard Stephens shouting his first name over and over, "Frederick, Frederick!"

Then Catherwood felt a strange vibrating sensation as he stood up. He first thought it was one of the frequent earthquakes. However the movement was followed by an overwhelming smell, a strong sulfur odor mixed with what could only be described as rotting flesh. He could barely keep from vomiting. He could see the porters and Stephens who was frantically talking to Arturo. The porters already had their packs filled with their belongings on their backs while Arturo began to pack his. Stephens was pleading for them to stay.

Catherwood with his lantern in hand approached Stephens when one of the porters grabbed him screaming, "Xibalba, Xibalba."

The terror in the porter's eyes was chilling as he turned, and Catherwood watched him run into the darkness. At that moment, he was suddenly knocked to the ground. Looking up he could see out of the corner of his eyes the remaining porters and the guide running after their friend all yelling, "Xibalba, Xibalba."

As Stephens helped him to his feet, Catherwood's only remarked, "What in bloody hell is Xibalba and why are they so afraid?"

Stephens reached and grabbed Arturo as he tried to streak by. He was babbling something over and over. The babbling soon became understandable to Stephens. "The Lords have awoken. The underworld is alive." That was the last they saw of Arturo as he, like the porters, disappeared into the jungle. The only acknowledgement of this frightening event appeared later in his journal referenced as "the superstitious beliefs of many of the local peasants."

CHAPTER 2

I know that sounds made up, but though those events really happened in the 19th century, it might help you to understand part of the exploration of Mayan ruins that Rosalia Canul had heard as a child.

The flight from Texas was over with no complications and surprisingly on time. Now she had to find her bus that would take her to Palenque, and this she knew would be the longest, most uncomfortable part of her trip. Rosalia was glad for the time to rethink her research plans and to prepare for her first trip home since Miguel, her maternal uncle, and his wife Izta had passed away. They had been like parents to her after he parents died in an automobile accident when she was five. Miguel and Izta had no children and the addition of Rosalia was seamless. Miguel was a respected Mayan guide and interpreter for scholars doing fieldwork in the area. He loved telling her stories and elaborating on Mayan legends, but Izta believed, as many Mayans, that some secrets of the ancients shouldn't be discussed. And she didn't want this new member of their family to wander and explore sacred areas for fear Rosalia would put herself in harm's way. Nevertheless, Rosalia remembered daily asking Miguel about stories of Mayan adventure and discovery.

As she learned in college, Miguel had been an assistant to Alberto Ruz Lhuillier in the 1940s after his direct involvement with the discovery of the tomb of Pakal, a Mayan king who ruled from 620-683; every new art historian and archeologist always hired him and, of course, deferred to his experience. Miguel was not a classically trained archeologist like Ruz, but due to his Mayan heritage with his language abilities to speak both Spanish and his naïve Quiche Mayan, he was an invaluable resource for researching scholars. He had tremendous respect for Ruz, especially the manner in which he treated the indigenous people like himself. Most researchers he had encountered treated native peoples as laborers. Ruz was born and educated in France, but after several years of archeological work in Mexico he fell in love with the country and its people. He became a Mexican citizen and fluent in Spanish. He never attempted to learn the difficult Mayan dialect spoken in Chiapas. The fact the Miguel knew the local language became the first essential bond between Ruz and Miguel.

After locating her bus to Palenque, Rosalia sat on it waiting for the driver to get enough passengers to leave. Patience was always needed since most transportation didn't run on an exact time schedule. The wait gave her time to think about how Miguel recounted the discovery of Pakal's tomb, one of Rosalia's favorite adventures that she asked her uncle to tell her over and over. It's so much more alive and meaningful to hear it from someone who was there, unlike the clinical recounting in texts.

It took place in the hills of Chiapas Altiplano, Mexico on June 15, 1952 when a group of archeologists lead by Alberto Ruz and accompanied by Miguel, begin the laborious job removing centuries of debris and rubble from the corbelled interior of a temple ruin in the ancient Mayan city of Palenque. The pyramidal structure was comprised of nine massive ascending platforms of earth meticulously faced in stone. It was a magnificently engineered building. After several days they finally had cleared the interior. Initially it appeared to mirror the interiors of the other temples at Palenque. While beautifully constructed there was nothing remarkable since all the ritual objects used by Mayan Lords and priests had long disappeared.

Within several minutes of inspection something on the floor caught Ruz's attention. A stone slab in the center of the temple's floor had a number of holes drilled into it and was cracked. This feature was unique.

His team threaded ropes through the drill holes and began lifting. When they removed the slab it, revealed two stone steps covered in debris. They began digging and removing the fill material, not knowing where this would lead them, or how deep they would have to go.

Ruz spent the next four seasons digging down beneath the floor of the Temple of the Inscriptions; they averaged approximately 20 steps a season. It was stifling hot and dangerous work clearing the steep narrow corbelled passage way that descended 73 steps down under the stone floor of the temple. The final removal of fill revealed a small square room. Disappointed, he turned to Miguel who was a skilled Mayan stonemason.

Ruz asked, "All these stairs for this?"

Miguel smiled and said, "Look at the small triangular stone on the wall. Why don't we remove that?"

Alberto, realizing they had nothing to lose, nodded his head. Within an hour they pried the stone out. It revealed a stone slab. They removed the rest of the masonry from the wall. It took all of them to levy the stone slab into the room.

Immediately there was a unified gasp and then everyone began speaking at the same time. Ruz asked for silence.

An enormous rectangular carved stone filled the newly revealed room.

Ruz looked over to Cesar who was both a friend and archeologist that had been assisting him on the final days of excavation.

Ruz questioned, "Is it an altar?"

Cesar thought out loud, "Why would they bury this 73 steps down in the middle of the temple?"

Miguel had advised Alberto to remove the triangular stone and now spoke, "Why don't we drill and see if it is hollow?"

That seemed logical to everyone. He began to drill and after an hour the drill bit seemed to start moving with more ease and then it pushed through without resistance. There was a slight peculiar odor that Alberto wondered to himself if it could be the burial remains of Pakal.

Everyone began to applaud and shout, "Bravo." As he started to back the drill bit out of the slab, it snapped wedged in the sarcophagus.

As exciting as this new discovery was, it left them with the daunting task of how to remove the lid. Alberto began to inspect the top of the 'altar.' Then he noticed that there was a slight gap between the massive block base and the top. He had no idea at the time how much the top weighed, but would later find that the 17'x11' slab weighed over five tons.

Smiling Miguel slowly said something in Mayan and then in Spanish, which bought an instant smile to Alberto's face.

"Tenemos un montón de gatos del automóvil!"

"We need a lot of automobile jacks."

Two hours later he appeared with fifteen jacks to lift the lid. It took several hours to set the jacks in place and devise a plan that would allow them to raise the massive lid in unison. Finally Ruz gave the command.

At first it seemed hopelessly stuck, then there was a loud pop like a seal had been broken. They began choking immediately as a strange putrid odor filled the chamber. Was this some sort of trap to protect the tomb? Before they could discuss what it was, the odor dissipated.

To their amazement, what they found would rival Howard Carter's discovery of King Tutankhamen's tomb thirty years earlier.

After Rosalia moved into her aunt and uncle's home, she became aware of what an extraordinary life her uncle had led. She had no idea how much he would impact her career and life. She would learn how amazing it was to be Mayan. The Mexican government had always treated her and her parents as second-class citizens, but now she had a new pride and respect for her cultural heritage. Of the many things she learned from her uncle, this would prove to be the ultimate gift.

The stories of Mayan discoveries and history influenced her playtime with the local children soon after arriving. They would spend the days exploring Palenque. They would alternate between pretending to be explorers and ancient Mayan historical figures. There was always a spirited argument as to who would play the role of the Mayan king, Pakal. The 'chosen one' would emerge from the tomb to be greeted by waiting attendants holding palm fronds. They would begin fanning the king as he made his way to the palace.

Izta was always worried about Rosalia playing at Palenque. She loved her aunt but always wondered how someone whose name meant 'dream' in Mayan could be so afraid of the magical wonders of Palenque. Izta, like the local elders, were superstitious since the opening of the tomb. Most were of traditional Mayan descent holding respect for the ancients' beliefs.

Pakal was an ancestral King and to disturb his tomb and peaceful afterlife was a sacrilege. This disturbance would interrupt his soul and its journey through Xibalba, the Mayan underworld. The past and the present were inextricably one and connected to all aspects of their daily lives.

Izta had forbidden her to go into the chamber since she still feared the spirit of Pakal would be angry. Her uncle knew she had frequently visited the tomb because she would always ask him new questions about specific aspects of the chamber, questions that indicated she had seen the inside. This always made him smile knowing she shared both the same interest and had a shared secret.

While her uncle was a hero in the world of archeology, locals still put him under suspicion for his part in the excavation. Every unexplainable occurrence, such as a rash of earthquakes followed by strange sulfur odors and animal caucuses found dismembered in the jungle were all attributed to the opening of the tomb and Pakal's displeasure. Similar reactions and suspicion occurred after the opening of King Tut-ankh-Amen's tomb.

Egyptian tombs and mummies had always fascinated Rosalia, especially the first words that were spoken by Howard Carter to Lord Carnarvon on that fateful day in 1922 when Carter finally broke through the wall of the antechamber of King Tut-ankh-Amen into the burial chamber. An anxious and excited Carnarvon couldn't stand the suspense any longer and asked Carter, "Can you see anything?"

Almost speechless Carter could only respond, "Yes, wonderful things."

His flashlight illuminated the interior of the only undisturbed burial chamber of a major king in the history of archeology. Of course, the next days Carter would discover unimaginable treasures of gold, including the burial coffin made of solid gold.

As spectacular as this seemed, it paled in comparison to her uncle's account of the day he and Ruz entered into the tomb chamber of the great Mayan Lord Pakal after four tireless years of digging. This uncovering was one of her favorite stories and was a frequent request that her uncle enjoyed telling her as much as she did listening to it over and over.

It would always start with the very moment he and Ruz broke through the tomb wall when a strange mist seemed to rush pass them, accompanied by a slight sound, almost a scream. The mist he remembered with a strange odor, not stale but like something rotting. They both gasped, but whatever they had just experienced became of little interest as they stepped into the chamber. Ruz later recalled to Miguel that out of the dim shadows emerged a vision as if from a fairy tale, a fantastic, ephemeral sight from another world. It seemed like a huge magic grotto carved out of ice, the walls sparkling and glistening like snow crystals. Delicate festoons of stalactites hung like tassels of a curtain, and the stalagmites on the floor looked like drippings from a great candle. The impression, in fact, was that of an abandoned chapel. Across the walls marched stucco figures in low relief, representing the Lords of Xibalba. When his eyes sought the floor, he noticed it was almost entirely filled with a great-carved stone slab in perfect condition.

He explained to Rosalia, " I tried to perceive it as the Palenque priests did when they were sealing it. I wanted to erase centuries and hear the last human voices that vibrated there. I struggled to understand the original message the ancient Mayans left behind. I was looking for the link between their lives and ours."

Then he would smile and recount how he told Ruz to drill a hole into what Ruz thought was an altar. Miguel's ingenuity never ceased to amaze her. The use of tire jacks was a solution that reminded her of a real life *Macgyver,* one of the few American TV problem solver heroes that was broadcasted in Palenque and translated into Spanish.

Raised a strict Catholic, Rosalia didn't really know much of Mayan history but was fascinated with the exotic and mysterious stories of Mayan religion. Her would read to her stories from what he referred to as their bible, *Popol Vuh*. A lot of the stories seemed strangely familiar; their creation myths and an epic flood were familiar to the Old Testament account in Genesis and the narrative of Noah.

However, there were underlying beliefs that were almost impossible to comprehend: the belief that when you died you would descend into a land called Xibalba ('she-bahl-bah'), meaning 'place of fear.' In the *Popol Vuh*, Xibalba is described as a court below the surface of the earth inhabited by souls of the deceased, a separate race of beings worshipping death and ruled by twelve gods. Their names were as frightening as Xibalba. The first, *One Death*, and his cohort *Seven Death* were the most senior and respected. The remaining ten Lords are often referred to as demons. Their responsibilities were focused on various forms of human suffering to cause sickness, starvation, fear, destitution, pain, and ultimately death. These Lords traditionally worked in pairs. Their names were even more ominous than their bosses. *Flying Scab* and *Gathered Blood*, sicken people's blood; *Pus Demon* and *Jaundice Demon* caused people's bodies to swell up; *Bone Staff* and *Skull Staff* turned dead bodies into skeletons; *Sweepings Demon* and *Stabbing Demon* would hide in the unswept areas of people's houses and stab them to death; *Wing* and *Packstrap* caused people to die coughing up blood while out walking on a road.

Wow! It made Catholic Purgatory and Hell seem like pleasant alternatives. She had always imagined Purgatory as a poorly decorated waiting room, located between heaven and hell where souls sat in silence waiting to find out their fates. At least they still had a chance, unlike the doomed of Xibalba. Anyone who entered Xibalba were subject to 'tests' designed by the lords—tests that seemed to Rosalia as cruel as anything Job encountered in the Old Testament "Book of Job.". The first test Satan did was to take away all of Job's animals, killing the servants that were with the animals, and killing all of Job's sons and daughters while they were eating together. Even though Satan did these things to Job, Job did not curse God like Satan had hoped Job would do.

The Lords of Xibalba were thought to inflict similar human suffering to humans when they least expected one of their tests. She wondered if she had ever passed by one of these Lords as she began to hold her Rosary tight to her chest; surely this would protect her. Rosalia would draw pictures of what she thought Xibalba and the Lords looked like. She had no way of knowing how accurate she was and what a horrible reunion she would have with her childhood artistic characters.

As horrifying as the Lords seemed, parts of *Popol Vuh* were both inspiring and epic, particularly the story of the two hero twins and their quest to find their father and uncle. As the story goes, their father and uncle had been summoned by the Lords to play a friendly ball game. The Lords, who cheated, defeated their father and uncle, and then sacrificed the men for their loss as an offering to their gods.

This was particularly interesting to her since in the description of Xibalba are the details of one of the most important structures, the ball court, where the Lords would play for the souls of the newly arrived. This really fascinated her since she and her friends, whose fathers were either the caretakers or guards, all respected her uncle and would allow them to play in the local ball court. She was the queen of Palenque, and she used her power to play a traditionally male only game. The court was a magical place. She and her friends would play "the ballgame" with a soccer ball trying to get the ball through the stone hoop markers located high up on either side of the sloping walls. It seemed impossible to understand how the Mayans, using a ball made out of solid latex, ever scored without the use of their hands or feet. If you were playing for your life knowing the loser would be sacrificed, maybe what seemed impossible was divinely inspired and assisted. One of the boys she played with would eventually climb up the sloping walls and push the ball through the marker screaming goal triumphantly and dedicating their victory to the fabled Pakal.

One day the hero Twins, Xbalanque and Hunahpu, were playing the ballgame like their father and uncle and were summoned to Xibalba by the Lords of the Underworld. The sound of ball bouncing infuriated the Lords since it hadn't occurred since their father and uncle had played. Rosalia always feared the twins might meet the same fate as their ancestors. As he read, her uncle would remind her that the twins would grow up to avenge their father and uncle. Being summoned was nothing like a gracious party invitation when her uncle recounted the amazing obstacles the twins encountered on their way to the Lords. They encountered trickery and trials before finally defeating the Lords of the Underworld in the ballgame. This always made her smile; what made her happiest was their reward of eternal life. They were transformed into sun and moon. Her uncle would always point to the heavens and say that's why the moon and the sun are constantly moving across the sky; the twins were still playing the ballgame.

CHAPTER 3

Rosalia could feel the memories of her childhood coupled with her apprehension of returning knowing that her aunt and uncle would not be there to greet her. The bus dropped her off at the only hotel near Palenque. It had been there since her childhood, but she noticed that there had been some major renovations; even the name had changed from the Hotel Palenque to The Mayan Imperial Hotel. What had been a series of modest bungalows of the Hotel Palenque was now a two-story structure with a surprisingly modern lobby. The woman behind the desk immediately recognized her. She was the mother of her childhood playmate, Efran. After a warm embrace and several minutes of catching up, Maria checked her in and gave Rosalia her keys. She was impressed that they now had keys to the rooms with an attached jade plaque bearing an engraved image of the burial mask of Pakal.

Maria smiled, "Beautiful, no? We have them made in China."

"Very classy and worthy of a Mayan Lord," smiled Rosalia.

It was a nice touch, given that jade was the most prized commodity among Mayan elite, offered to the gods in ritual sacrifices and buried during the dedications of temples. After Rosalia got settled, a small commuter bus picked her up to take her to her childhood playground and one of the ancient Mayan archeological 'Wonders of the World.' It was a new Ford van, a big change from the old school bus: however, the road still had a familiar rhythm. She almost anticipated the bumps. The van driver was a young Mayan woman not much older than she. Rosalia watched her amazing smile in the mirror and then focused on the crucifix gently swaying around her neck.

She had always admired the conviction of native Mayans to openly accept Catholicism and still practice their ancient Mayan beliefs. This synthesis of cultures had fascinated her since childhood and her graduate studies only reinforced the similarities between the ancient Mayan *Popol Vuh* (Book of the People) and the Old Testament, particularly the Book of Genesis. As a Catholic, the acceptance of two cultural creation beliefs seemed to her a religious conflict.

Her favorite memories were immediately reinforced as she got out of the bus to the entrance where 3 local children were waiting for their next tourist victim. One had the ubiquitous Chiclets gum, the gum of choice in Guatemala. The other had what she assured Rosalia were authentic Mayan ceramic figures, all clearly marked with a sticker "Made in Guatemala." She purchased the fruit flavored Chiclets and a small replica of Pakal's funerary mask that now rounded out her Pakal collection to 9 along with a range of reproductions in varying sizes and quality of Lord Pakal's sarcophagus lid.

She was attracted, however, to the young boy selling Copal incense. She asked him if he actually had any of the real Copal sap from the Mayan Lords most sacred tree. He smiled and in Mayan replied, "Yes." As a child she had sold tourists many of the same items, but Copal was something that only the visiting archeologists understood and requested. Copal is a pungent sap when exposed to the air becomes hardened. When burned, it was the most sacred ritual offering Mayan Lords would offer the gods, except for the blood of their foreskins. Copal, the 'blood' of trees, was primarily food for deities. Maize was the human counterpart, food that nurtured life.

When she was a child, Rosalia and her friends would sell tourists Copal and other items. She picked up a small piece. Pretending not to know what Copal was used for she asked, "What is this?"

The boy replied, "Copal!"

"Is it a rock?"

"No it is sap from a tree."

"What is it used for?"

Rosalia listened in delight as he patiently explained to her the importance of Copal to the Mayan peoples.

"The smoke from burning Copal provided a link between their world and the sacred world. Not only did the smoke provide the imagery of the vision quest, like seeing forms in the clouds, but its smell was exactly like that of blood burning. The most sacred of offering of Mayan Kings."

She was impressed by his knowledge.

"What are you asking for it?"

"20 pesos."

Rosalia took out a 50 peso coin.

Rosalia smiled and said, "Thank you and keep the change."

His smile was infectious.

The odor was beautifully sweet and pungent. She had always preferred the sap to the alternative. It so reminded her of the beautiful silver incense orbs Catholic priests swing in procession while the smoke rises in rhythm down the nave of the cathedral.

She made her way to the site and descended the familiar 73 steps. She had an almost out of body experience as though she was on an escalator moving through time and space. Then she became aware of small details that had only seemed as architectural necessities. The 13-corbelled vaults had new meaning. Like the exterior 9 platforms of the temple, which had long been thought to represent the 9 levels of Xibalba, she realized 13-corbels represented the 13 levels of heaven. She realized she was at the nexus of the cosmos and underworld.

Pakal and his sons had built a replica of the Mayan underworld, complete with a mountain in the form of the temple, a cave in the form of the tomb and the essential river to the underworld and the sarcophagus laid on top of the portal to Xibalba.

There are sacred sites in the Yucatan where all three of these—the mountain, the cave and the river—occurred naturally with mountains made of limestone, shaped like Mayan temples, and at their base, caves in which underground rivers flow. Rosalia remembered numerous Mayan ritual objects were discovered in the caves including many examples of pottery distinctly from Palenque. It is possible that Pakal might have made pilgrimages to perform rituals since for centuries Mayans have still actively used this site.

As she entered the tomb chamber she became even more appreciative, even though most of the original materials—Pakal's remains, his funerary garments, jewelry, including his ruler rings, greenstone pieces, and a magnificent jade mask that covered his face were installed in a faithful recreation model of the tomb in the National Museum of Anthropology and History. She had a complete overview thanks to several photos taken by Ruz in the 1950s and the Museum installation drawings. The tomb was an installation that no museum could fully recreate. Pakal's remains had been ritually placed in a 23' x 12.2' foot chamber, hand painted with red hieroglyphs, carved borders and a huge monolith at the top that sealed the sarcophagus.

Nine richly dressed characters were carved on the chambers walls; something that the museum decided would compromise their condition if removed. She walked around the tomb as she greeted the brilliantly colored "Nine Night Masters," rulers of the Nine Underworld Levels and protectors of Pakal that would accompany Pakal through his transition to the underworld. At the last section of the hall there were two reproductions of Pakal's funerary mask that represented his face; in Maya culture this guaranteed that his image would remain beyond death.

For Rosalia the "Nine Masters" and Pakal's masks were similar to the "stations of the cross," each marking a pivotal moment in Christ's sufferings on his journey to his crucifixion. Like most Catholics during Lent, Rosalia would faithfully stop at each of the 14 station images lining the walls of the cathedral to say prayers for the sufferings and insults that Jesus endured during his passion.

To her Catholic background knowledge, the sarcophagus was a sepulcher marking Christ's final resting place before his journey. Unlike Christ's undecorated burial, the monumental Pakal sarcophagus and its richly decorated lid could not be removed due to its size and weight. How insightful of Pakal's sons! Pakal's skeletal remains, stunning jade burial mask, and other burial materials were removed in modern times as a safety precaution but still his presence was palpable to Rosalia. The sarcophagus lid was her love; it was comprised of a monolithic 5-ton stone rectangle while the sarcophagus itself weighing 15-tons. On its top was an exquisitely carved image of Pakal as a child, rising into the sky as the newborn maize god and ascending skyward to the east on a magnificent jade tree, representing life renewal. Portraits of his ancestors were depicted around the four sides of the coffin, each figure with a headdress representing a specific fruit tree.

Rosalia was exhilarated and felt her uncle's encouraging presence as well as the warnings of her aunt to leave the dead alone. Anticipating tomorrow, she was confident Anthony Michael would help her unravel the mysteries of the tomb.

CHAPTER 4

She climbed the familiar stairs of the tomb and returned to the hotel to meet Anthony in the small hotel bar at 6:00 P.M. She had never met him, but thought she could recognize him from the small photo on the jacket of his book, *Mayan Art as History*.

She got to the bar a half hour early, sat facing the lobby that was fairly busy with tourist, and ordered a gin and tonic. She looked at her watch and as the hand struck 6.00pm she looked up. She was not disappointed when she noticed he was as handsome as the photo, However, she began giggling when noting he was wearing what in the trade was referred to as the Banana Republic field research suit, an all khaki experience.

Anthony was a little intimidating at first, his knowledge of her work, particularly her dissertation, was commanding. At first she wasn't sure he was trying to impress her or impress himself. She was soon relieved to sense he was actually a little intimidated by her.

Rosalia asked, "Didn't you fly here directly from a dig on which you were a consultant."

"Yes, archaeologists were excavating temples and pyramids in the village of Tahtzibichen in Mérida, the capital of Yucatán states. They discovered a 1,900-year-old vessel on which there were several unique features. The traditional priest and king figures had been replaced with an elaborate text/ glyph sequence with a reference to Palenque. I thought you might know why a vessel hundreds of miles away seems to have such a direct connection to Pakal?"

Rosalia was curious since the 750C.E. date was also significant, with Pakal's death having been established at 683C.E. Why would Mayans commemorate a King from Chiapas 60 years after his death? Thinking about these curiosities, Rosalia asked him, "So you found something unique about the glyph system at Tahtzibichen, particularly the subject, Pakal"?

Anthony was surprised, since he had only told her that there were similarities in the glyph sequence similar to the ones on the sarcophagus; he had never mentioned the Pakal connection. Obviously, she was well connected and had friends on the dig.

He smiled and nodded. She knew she had established her familiarity with his site.

He immediately changed the subject. "I can't even begin to understand what it would be like to have grown up here, to be able to speak the language and to know the customs. Rosalia, I had a difficult time learning Spanish for my graduate research. I'm especially impressed by your ability to decipher the glyphs."

"Read the glyphs. Sorry, I am a little sensitive since reading to me seems as though I am still in direct communication with my ancestors."

"That's exactly why I need your help. As you have already noted this discovery on this vessel is unusual given the Pakal reference and distance of Tahtzibichen from Palenque."

"Yes, not to mention the dates of the pottery vessel implying its creation 60 years after his death," responded Rosalia.

Anthony couldn't let this one go by. "O.K. how do you know all of this? Who do you know on the dig?"

Rosalia wasn't about to give up her source. She was having too much fun with him and her new found power. "Don't worry. I won't tell anyone so your discovery is safe with me."

Archeologists and Art Historians are notoriously secretive about their research. The ultimate unveiling, particularly of something as important as this, would be to coordinate the publication date in conjunction with a major conference. In such a setting, Anthony could stand in front of his admiring peers, see the look of amazement on their faces and hear the thundering round of applause that was sure to follow. Then he would announce that they would be able to read his full account in his new book available in bookstores the following week. The drama couldn't get any better.

He smiled nervously; he was clearly uncomfortable that Rosalia immediately picked up on it.

"Don't worry, he's not in the academic field. One of the native workers is the son of my uncle's oldest friend, and he knew I would be interested," responded Rosalia.

The smile returned to his face and he hoped his discovery was safe.

They agreed to meet at 6:00 A.M. at the hotel's entrance the next morning to visit the site.

CHAPTER 5

The Journey Begins

Anthony didn't let her down; he was dressed for an expedition in khaki, hiking boots and a backpack worthy of an assault on Mt. Everest. She smiled.

He immediately noticed she was wearing a bright yellow pair of capris and royal blue blouse with her favorite tropical footwear, Teva river sandals. Functional and stylish, it couldn't have been any better. The colors looked radiant against her dark skin.

The cab arrived on time for the fifteen minute ride to Palenque. When they arrived, she made Anthony repeat her routine of purchasing lime flavored Chiclets, another Pakal mask for her collection and an unusually large piece of Copal sap. She assured him he would become addicted to the smell.

Anthony was overwhelmed as they got close enough to see the legendary tower of the palace, something he had only seen in books and in Powerpoint symposium presentations by scholars that had been there. It was a particularly impressive engineering feat in the New World, of four separate floors connected by a series of stairs.

Rosalia could see his excitement as they walked around the site. Anthony's pace started to accelerate when they began descending to the tomb. Rosalia loved his energy.

As soon as they began to go down the stairs Anthony stopped and took his backpack off. He began to take some of the contents out. Anthony was well equipped. His backpack seemed to include an endless inventory of gadgets that art historians who had seen the movie *Indiana Jones*, would want to have included on their wish list. Indy was so cool but at the same time fairly low tech: however he was able to solve and encounter incredible obstacles and situations with very few resources. Anthony, on the other hand, had an amazing array of cutting edge boy toys. Among the most ridiculous she thought were the infrared goggles he put on as they entered the tomb.

On the sides of the lid were her favorite images of the elaborate glyphs and their phonetic counter parts. The combined image and text didn't get any better for deciphering meaning. The glyphs had long been the interest of scholars especially since the work of Tatiana in the late 1960s revealed that most Mayan art related to what she referred to as a king's list, a compulsive record of Mayan Genealogy. This was especially important in understanding the tomb of Pakal. His accomplishments and genealogy were beautifully and eternally recorded in low relief around the entire border of the sarcophagus. For Rosalia this was an exceptional moment. Pakal was speaking to her and she so wanted to begin their dialogue. Her wish would come true.

As she reread the glyphs for Anthony, she became aware that the sequence that she had become so familiar with was somehow different. She put her halogen headlamp on that she thought was technologically the best innovation in archeology since thermolumonesece dating methods for ceramics. The name glyph for Pakal was repeated which was not unusual; however the phonetic sign pronouncing his name was also repeated. This had somehow been overlooked. The Mayan genealogies were always repetitious referring to the composition/order of the descendant's bloodline.

But as she read through the sequence, Pakal's name, "the shield," seemed to be stressed more than his blood ancestors. The namesake "shield" wasn't a metaphor but the literal translation of shield or protector. She pointed to the glyph. Anthony knelt down. She could see his profile out of the corner of her eye, and his goggles reminded her of the stylized images of the lords painted on the sides of Mayan pottery with their eyes bulging, almost popping out of their heads. She had to hold back her laughter.

"I know this sounds compulsive," remarked Anthony but I brought along a second pair of the goggles. After you made fun of me I thought you wouldn't be interested, but I really think you really need to see this. The difference is amazing."

She felt that the light in the tomb had always seemed adequate, a few incandescent bulbs and her halogen head lamp was like a torch, illuminating everything in the direction her head turned. However, the immediacy of his voice, told her to take him up on his offer to try the night goggles. She put them on reluctantly. Immediately she was amazed at the difference. It was as though she was seeing the tomb for the first time. It was vibrant.

"Wow!"

Anthony smiled with pride and satisfaction for his forethought.

After surveying the interior and lifting the goggles from her eyes and putting them back on several times Rosalia was converted. She knelt down and began to scrutinize the glyph sequence and she realized for the first time that the 2nd repetition of the glyph was in higher relief and seemed to have an edge that almost looked like it was a separate piece of stone, set into a recess like a part of a jigsaw puzzle. Given the normal lighting conditions, this would have easily been overlooked in the past.

"Rosalia, what's up?"

"Anthony, something has changed since the last time I was here."

"How is that possible? This has been here since Pakal's son's laid him to rest."

"No, the glyph sequence has a change."

"Now you are beginning to worry me. Those are carved in stone. Has someone come back and recarved them since you were here last?"

Rosalia looked at him; her expression said it all. She made Antony kneel down beside her.

Anthony's glyph knowledge was at an introductory 101 level. Rosalia realized she had to be patient with him, particularly given he was the only person within miles that could even begin to understand the importance of what she thought she had discovered.

"Look at these glyphs," she demanded.

"They appear to be identical."

"Good. They are."

"Why are they repeated in such close proximity to each other?"

"That's not unusual," she said, thinking how typical of an art historian when considering all object and no substance. She was generalizing, of course, but sometimes the medium was the message, and in this case it was the script. She really wished her uncle was here.

"So what? I thought I was doing pretty good," smiling at her. She returned the gesture.

"Now really. Look at the two symbols. Notice any difference?" she insisted.

Anthony really studied the two to see what she was seeing, and then in an inspired moment he looked at her.

Rosalia immediately noticed his expression. "O.K., what is it?" she asked.

"It is much more defined."

"What do you mean defined?"

"More deeply carved, higher relief, all the other glyphs are the same relief."

"Exactly," she reaffirmed.

"So what is the significance?"

"I'm not sure."

CHAPTER 6

Rosalia took her pocketknife out. She swung the small blade out. Anthony looked on incredulously as she began to probe and scratch around the edges of the glyph.

"This never happened," she said.

"I wish it wasn't happening," Anthony responded.

As she cleared the encrusted dirt from around the edges, she could see that it was actually a separate piece. She tried pulling to see if it would come out, no movement. Anthony looked on.

"Are sure you know what you are doing?"

"Not a clue, but what else could I try?"

"Push," Anthony suggested. Immediately she tried his suggestion. The sound was a deafening whoosh, like a massive vacuum opening creating a gust of wind. As the "shield" glyph pushed in, the room began to vibrate and the sarcophagus began to slide back with the wall depicting the reliefs of the lords moving with it. The smell was overwhelming. They both began to gag.

Rosalia reached out to Anthony. They clutched tightly. They stood frozen for what seemed forever. Panic couldn't begin to describe the fear that was pulsating through their bodies.

Finally each got their breath back.

"Maybe Erich von Daniken wasn't that crazy. The sarcophagus lid actually depicts Lord Pakal at the controls of a space ship and extraterrestrials were responsible for most archeological phenomena and we are about to blast off," thought Rosalia out loud.

"Are you alright?" asked Anthony.

She nodded

"Are you?"

"I don't know how to begin to answer that. If you mean *am I alive then*, yes I am alright."

While they never communicated to each other they were immediately appreciative that the incandescent lights that had illuminated the interior were still working. Somehow that seemed an important link between their newly defined underworld and the world they already longed for the stairs that led them there.

Rosalia was strangely comforted to see how truly shaken he was; her fears were reinforced as acceptable. As though choreographed they both removed their goggles. They seemed even more uncomfortable, given the temperature was noticeably hotter.

Maybe they had really opened the underworld. If that was the case their situation didn't feel, smell or look good.

"Please tell me you have something in your backpack that will make this better," pleaded Rosalia.

"You mean a gas mask?"

She looked at him hopefully as he shook his head.

"Altoid Mint is about the best I can do. Maybe put one in each nostril."

She laughed nervously.

They both turned their heads toward the cavernous hole that was revealed beneath the sarcophagus. The vision goggles were of little help seeing through what appeared to be dense fog. The halogen flashlights only bounced the light back into their eyes.

Rosalia was the first to notice that their new discovery wasn't the worst of their problems. The sarcophagus was now blocking the stairwell; what had been their exit strategy was now hopelessly sealed. It would appear that it was designed so that as the new portal was revealed the old one was sealed: an amazing engineering accomplishment.

"What do we do?" she asked.

"What are our options?"

"We could wait to see if someone up there can help us."

"The tomb is sealed I doubt that anyone could hear us, let alone move that stone," Anthony said.

"Maybe there is a button on the outside. You know a magic glyph that reads 'In case of emergency, push'."

Her attempt at humor was acknowledged with a slight smile. The only way to go was a set of stairs revealed by the sarcophagus sudden repositioning.

"It would appear that our only way out is down," said Anthony reluctantly.

She shook her head in agreement.

"We need a plan. All we know at this point is we have a hole in the floor that we can't see into," noted Rosalia.

"You mean we need a Xibalba strategy?"

"Exactly. Let's go over what we know about Xibalba," suggested Rosalia.

"Where do we start? The *Popol Vuh* is 500 pages; we need Cliff's notes."

"Let's focus on physical aspects. You know the descriptions of the terrain, the barriers, tests, etc?" hoped Rosalia.

"You mean a guide book?"

Rosalia began to smile, "Yes."

Anthony took out a small notebook that he had intended to write the answers and observations that his beautiful guide was to have provided as they inspected the tomb. How wonderful that tomb experience would have been!

They spent several hours, remembering and reviewing the major points of the *Popol Vuh* to the best of their collective abilities. At times they would finish each other's sentences.

Finally it was time.

"Do you think there is a ladder, steps, a rope?" asked Anthony.

"They never mention that part. The souls are placed in the setting of Xibalba, and how they actually descend into that realm is a mystery."

"I have rope," he offered in hopes of contributing a solution.

As he pointed to the rope, she remembered seeing it that morning hanging from his backpack as he placed it into the trunk of the taxi. She really thought it was silly, given that all they were going to do was spend day in Pakal's tomb that his sons had so thoughtfully included a stairwell for convenience. Why the rope, she had thought at the time.

He took the rope and tied one end to a steel reinforcement bar that had been installed by Ruz to help his crew with the leverage necessary in moving the massive sarcophagus lid for the first time. He then began tying knots at 2' intervals.

Rosalia was impressed with his initiative.

CHAPTER 7

"Can you climb a rope? Where did you learn to do this?" she wanted to know.

He smiled, "Boy Scouts".

He began lowering the rope. It disappeared immediately.

"I am going to leave the backpack here, just to be safe."

Rosalia's face began to tremble. She held back the tears welling up in her eyes.

"I am only going down a little ways, just a test run," he said

She smiled encouragingly.

He put his goggles on and placed the small halogen flash light in his mouth, clenching it between his teeth.

He sat with his legs dangling into the hole.

"I will be right back."

"Please make sure you are."

He grasped the first knot with both his hands, slowly lowering himself. It was an odd illusion as the mist began engulfing him and his body disappeared. In a moment he was gone, out of view.

She gasped.

"What do you see?"

There was no answer.

She began screaming his name. No answer. Several minutes passed and she was sure he would never return. She would slowly die, suffocating, as the little remaining air ran out.

She tried pulling on the rope. There was definitely still resistance. Was it Anthony or were the Lords pulling on it, trying to pull her into their world?

She went to the edge of the sarcophagus to sit and contemplate the inevitable. It seemed ironic that place of her academic affection would become her resting place.

She stared at the hole and regretted that she had noticed the relief difference of the shield glyph. What was she thinking taking her knife and probing? Her thoughts were interrupted by a familiar sight, that hat that she had made so much fun of was slowly emerging from the fog, And to her delight it was sitting atop Anthony's head. He smiled.

As he finally climbed out of the abyss, she hugged him.

"Why didn't you answer me?"

"I did. Why didn't you answer me?"

"I did."

Then Anthony explained, "The fog not only acts as a visual barrier but a sound shield."

"What is down there? What did you see?"

"I climbed about 15' and I felt what I thought was ground. As my head literally got out of the fog I saw that I was on a ledge. Thank god for the goggles."

"A ledge. Over what?"

"I have good news, well relatively speaking. I think that it is only 30' from the ledge to the ground."

"What about the fog?"

"The fog seems to be concentrated around the entrance of the hole."

He looked at her, as she seemed to almost be relieved at his news.

Rosalia gestured to the hole.

"Shall we?"

Anthony put on his backpack and Rosalia her goggles.

"Let me go first. I can steady the rope at the bottom."

They both sat on the edge with their legs dangling over.

He grasped the rope and soon disappeared, this time she had none of the fear from his last disappearing act. About a minute passed and she felt a tug on the rope. It was her signal to begin. Slowly and cautiously she began, grasping the rope, scooting off the edge and as he had instructed her then using her legs to leverage her descent.

Anthony was relieved to see her Teva's appearing from the fog, and then Rosalia's smile as her entire body came out of the mist.
He steadied her.
"Welcome to Xibalba."

It was nothing like she could have ever expected or been prepared for.
It appeared as a vast void, moonscape, seemingly flat and eternal or 'a forever distance' or was that the visual effect of the goggles.

Anthony didn't say a thing since he had just had the same experience he wanted her to take it in so they could talk about it without him influencing her impressions. She took off her goggles and immediately put them on just as he had done.
"Well?"
"Pitch black."
"Incredible, huh?"
"Incredible, yes. How do we get down? The rope is still tied to the tomb."
"I forgot to tell you up there that when I looked over the edge, after a few seconds, I could see a stone ladder."
"Wonderful. I don't think I could handle a 30' rope experience after that."
"Well it's not literally a ladder in the true sense."
"What do you mean? A ladder is a ladder, doesn't matter if it is made of stone."
"Do you know what toe-and-hand-holes are?"
"You mean like the wounds Jesus received on the cross?"
Anthony tried not to laugh.
"No, no, the kind that Ancestral Puebloans used."
She shrugged her shoulders.

"I grew up in southwestern Colorado in a small town named Mancos."

"Yes, what does that have to do with Xibalba?"

"I know you have heard of Mesa Verde."

"The cliff dwellings, so what?"

"As a child growing up that was my Palenque. My friends and I would hike up the canyons and avoid the park ranger and the tourist bus tours. Since most of the access to the sites today is via paths, stairs and ladders provided by the park service, we had to improvise. We soon noticed that most of the ruins had a series of concave imprints that were exactly the distance of our hand and foot patterns, literally a ladder for your toes and hands. We became extremely adept at using the ancient system."

She looked over the ledge. It took a while, then she noticed a series of depressions alternating from right to left in an amazing rhythm; she realized this was his so-called ladder. The rope seemed like a luxury.

Her expression said it all. He immediately tried to assure her that it was going to be all right.

"I will go down first and you will be right behind me. I can walk you through it,"

He immediately realized that was the wrong phrase, so he rephrased it.

"I can talk you through it. You can watch me and then repeat what I do; I will only be a couple of feet from you, and the best news, no fog. I can use the remaining rope to tether us together in case you slip. Trust me."

She didn't speak. Simply nodded.

Anthony lowered himself over the edge, his foot gratefully connected with the foot hole. He then alternated foot to hand and was 10' down.

"O.K. Rosalia, come on down."

Very cautiously she grabbed the edge and lowered herself down. This was, she thought, the most adventurous and stupid thing she had ever attempted. Given the circumstances, it was a *fait accompli*.

She was completely engaged in the face of the cliff, almost feeling confident, when she heard Anthony call. "Stop. Stop!"

"What. What's wrong? I am O.K."

"I'm not."

"What do you mean?"

"It has been coded, encrypted with a security program."

"What do you mean?"

"Like Mesa Verde, the ladders have a specific beginning sequence, which foot right or left begins the pattern. If you start with the wrong one you, become, as they say, wrong footed. Can't go down or up. Stuck."

"Yes"

"That's where I am, I can't move, the next step is 25' down."

All of a sudden her adrenaline kicked in.

She began to climb back up.

"What are you doing?"

"Please be quiet."

She got back to the last hand hole before the ledge, grabbed the ledge and, in a feat of incredible confidence and strength, pulled herself to the safety of the ledge.

She looked down at Anthony.

"I am going to pull you back up."

"No offense, but how?"

"I'm going to tie the rope to my waist and pull while you climb. We can do it."

Each step seemed a labor, but in a matter of minutes Anthony had joined her on the ledge.

Again they hugged. This seemed to be a tradition after a near disaster, and while it was comforting, the frequency of near disasters was becoming alarming. After resting for several minutes, they agreed to make another attempt.

"We need to agree which foot we both started on last time, which one we put into the hole first so that doesn't happen again," Anthony said.

"I have an idea so there is no confusion, or power of suggestion. Let's put our hands behind our backs and make a fist with the right or left hand depending on which one we remember starting with."

"Great."

Two right-handed fists appeared.

The descent was truly uneventful.

As they reached the ground, it felt somehow reassuring.

They stood and after a moment Rosalia said, "Something is missing."

"The dog?"

"Yes, our canine guide."

According to Maya myth, the souls of the dead had to follow a dog with night vision on a horrific and watery path and endure myriad challenges before they could rest in the afterlife. The problem was that the Lords of Xibalba weren't expecting them, and their canine guide wasn't waiting for them.

"They don't know we are here. I guess the good news is that we are not souls," said Rosalia with a smile.

"It would appear that the living are on their own." Rosalia nodded.

She removed her goggles. At first it was pitch black, then her eyes began to adjust. It was dark, yet things seemed to almost have luminosity to them. Like the creatures National Geographic scientists photographed at the bottom the ocean, they had that same iridescent quality.

Her initial impressions of Xibalba were almost numbing. As her eyes adjusted to the blue iridescent glow, the landscape started to come into focus. Everything appeared in high definition like wearing 3D glasses at a movie. The flat ground glowed under her feet. It seemed endless with only occasional rock formations. Everything seemed so real and tangible, which in itself was a contradiction, since everything she was witnessing never existed in her world; yet it was so real.

Anthony took off his backpack. Opening the side compartment, he took out a small camera.

Rosalia asked, "What are you taking a picture of?"

"I'm not sure, but I just feel we should document all of this."

He started clicking away. After several clicks he stopped.

Frustrated, Anthony exclaimed, "The damn flash doesn't work. My camera broke right before the trip. I borrowed my brother's. Well I just didn't think about checking it."

Rosalia looked at the small view screen, "Well there is a slight glow. You caught something. Maybe something can be done with Photo Shop or some other computer program when we get back."

Anthony's disappointment was still evident.

She could see what she thought were trees in the distance, the only form that penetrated the distant horizon. As they began walking they, became aware of the unusual quality of the ground. Their feet sank into the surface leaving footprints that looked like the molds made by forensic officers investigating a murder. Rosalia was the first to notice that each of their imprints disappeared with each new step. As she looked back, she saw that any trace of their presence was erased, and as she thought to herself, so had those of all who had come before them.

They walked for what seemed hours. Anthony glanced at his watch, surprised only an hour had passed since they began their journey. Either the watch wasn't working or time somehow had slowed dramatically.

Rosalia asked, "Could we stop and rest?"

"Of course."

They sat on the ground; the sand was more like dry silt that conformed to their bodies. Anthony took out his canteen and offered it to Rosalia. She sipped sparingly realizing that it was their only water supply until they found a new one. Given the terrain around them that didn't seem likely in the near future. Anthony took his backpack off and unzipped one of the outer compartments. He handed Rosalie a zip lock bag. It was filled with the quintessential archeology staple, trail mix. Never had granola, raisins and almonds tasted so good.

CHAPTER 8

Almost in unison they got up and began walking. Rosalia looked back and, as before, there were no traces or imprints of where they had rested. In the distance was a series of what appeared to be an army of tall thin figures, standing perfectly still as though they were at attention. They stopped and for a few minutes surveyed these strange sentinels. They began to approach cautiously monitoring for any sign of movement. Soon they realized that they were looking at what seemed to be a petrified forest.

"They are the "Match Stickmen," said Rosalia.

"Are you talking about the song?"

"What are you talking about?" she responded.

"What you're talking about. I thought you were referring to the song *Pictures of Matchstickmen* by the 1960s British group, "Status Quo.""

"I have no idea what you are talking about, "answered Rosalia. "We didn't hear a lot of the British invasion where I grew up!"

They both began laughing realizing how silly their exchange had been.

"The wooden men, you know the ones from the creation myth! You know like Genesis; in this case the creator gods called the "Heart of Heaven" tried in several failed attempts to create living beings to praise and venerate them. Corn meal was the first and it soon turned to mush after the rains, then wooden beings which were like marionettes without the ability to think let alone exalt their creators."

Anthony smiled "Well you could say that the Adam and Eve experiment didn't go as planned either.

As they walked through the forest of figures they noticed that they all seemed to be in different positions as though in an instant the "Heart of Heaven" had quickly aborted their attempt as their wooden puppets began crashing into one another. In an odd way it reminded Anthony of the 10,000 terracotta warriors discovered in 1974 in Shaanxi China in the tomb of the first Qin Emperor. They were created in the 3rd century B.C.E. to provide eternal protection, however when unearthed not one of the life size soldiers came to his protection. As they worked through the fringe of the of the forest they were immediately confronted by what looked like a large rock outcropping in the distance. Their flat lunar landscape was becoming unexpectedly interesting. As they got closer the rock started to transform.

Anthony was the first to speak."The Sleeping Ute."

Rosallia responded, "Now you are starting to sound like me. Is this a 'Status Quo' reference?"

"No, when I was growing up in the Cortez area of Colorado, I had always been fascinated with the mountain range I could see from my bedroom window of the profile of the legendary Sleeping Ute. To the local Native American culture it was a sacred icon of a reclining hero; it was magical to see something so ancient on such a gargantuan scale.

As they got closer, the strange silhouette of the rocks started to change. It began to take on the form of an enormous seated figure.

Rosallia and Anthony spoke at the same time. "Seven Macaw."

They realized that their earlier suspicions were right; they were retracing the journey of the hero twins through Xibalba. Seven Macaw was the first obstacle that the twin' encountered: a gigantic seated being, who sat right in the path of the twins quest. When they approached, the figure became animated as though it had been awakened from a deep sleep. Slowly it began to stir, the vacant eyes started to glow a faint green light and then like a lighthouse they became beacons. In an instant they turned to the twins, temporarily blinding them.

It spoke. "Who are you? How dare you approach the Sun God."

The Hero twins had been warned by "Heart of Sky" that Seven Macaw unhappy with his fate in the terrestrial world, had descended into Xibalba and proclaimed himself the Sun God, since the job was already taken in the heavens. There was no one to challenge him. He had the "old ones" replace his eyes and teeth with jewels. He looked resplendent and to those on their journey must have truly looked like a god. The twins were able to fool him and through a series of tricks they removed his teeth and eyes and replaced them with quartz and corn. The pride of Seven Macaw soon died and he became only a boulder in the crossroads of Xibalba.

Anthony smiled as he thought, "light out, nobody home" but he didn't think that Rosalia would be impressed with his little joke.

"I can only hope that the rest of the obstacles that the twins encountered will be as uneventful as ours was with "Seven Macaw," Rosalia said hopefully.

Anthony nodded.

They could only hope that all of the other tests were dormant. This is the first time that an "out of order sign," would be welcome.

CHAPTER 9

They could see in the distance a slight rise, approaching they could make out a ridge then they heard the first sounds since they had entered Xibalba. At first it reminded her of maracas' with percussion back up group. However, there was none of the distinct rhythms only discordant chattering. And as they got closer it sounded more like the high impedance of metal objects scraping against one another. She began thinking back to her uncle and the Popol Vuh stories. And in a sudden frightening moment she realized what they were about to encounter. At first it looked like a river with the most beautiful water currents moving in waves, like individual drops moving and undulating. They looked at each other at the same time, then screamed "river of scorpions." The riverbanks were littered with skeletons, obviously the preferred diet. They could only imagine how many more were underneath the scorpion hoards. They seemed to move like worker ants, more robotic in a mindless dance. It was frighteningly hypnotic.

They retreated to what they hoped was a safe distance. This was determined by establishing an arbitrary periphery between them and the skeletons with a ratio factor based on the interminable speed that the scorpions were moving. In this case it was approximately 300 yards. Truly this was high school algebra gone bad.

"Does this also seem strangely familiar?"

"Yes, the second test, only this one seems to be alive and well."

Anthony smiled, "Welcome to Xibalba, the Lords have certainly spared no expense."

Rosalia smiled, "You want to know what is so cool about this? We are being given the same reception as the twins."

"Are we are really the living Popol Vuh? If that's the case I would rather be a footnote," Anthony noted.

Anthony had hoped that the Seven Macaw encounter would set the precedent for what was to come in that he and Rosalia would be witness to the ruins of Xibalba and, like tourists, they would visit the ancient sites that the twins had. They could imagine each of the epic struggles that the Hero's endured, kind of like touring the archeological sites in *Homer's Iliad and Odyssey,* and bring to life Odysseus's adventures. What was happening however was a little too real.

Rosalia asked Anthony, "Do you remember how they get across this river?"

"No, please tell me you remember!"

"I can only remember that they don't get stung; it never says how they accomplished a successful crossing."

"Not even in a footnote?" Anthony said hoping.

They decided to edge closer to the river to see if there was a clue.

Rosalia remembered, "Did you notice how when we both screamed the scorpions didn't move towards us?"

"Yes, but do you even know if scorpions can hear?"

Rosalia smiled and shrugged her shoulders.

"Are you willing to take a chance, Rosalia?"

"Don't you think we have already gone beyond that?"

Anthony walked over to one of the skeletons and picked a bone up, then threw it directly into the river. Rosalia gasped. As they watched, their horrific expectations didn't occur. Not only didn't the bone excite the scorpions turning them in a stampede towards them, the bone didn't even bounce off of them. It simply seemed to vanish. They looked at each other.

Rosalia quickly realized what was happening and blurted out, "It's an illusion."

"One of the lord's tricks," Anthony confirmed.

Rosalia deduced, "That means all these skeletons were the people too frightened to try."

They took each other's hand and walked toward what they now hoped was an illusion. They were surprised that not only were the scorpions not real but their expectation of stepping down into the river was also an illusion. It was simply flat. Their feet and legs displaced the flow pattern of the scorpions as they walked to the river's bank. It was an exceptional display of the power and wizardry of the lords.

Anthony sighed, " I feel relieved to have that behind us!"

"When was the last time you read the Popol Vuh?" asked Rosalia, wondering if he remembered what was still ahead.

He smiled. "I know what's ahead."

CHAPTER 10

Several uneventful hours had passed as they walked though what was now a familiar landscape. They would soon realize that, like the Hero Twins, the challenges would start happening in rapid order. Rosalia was the first to notice. She looked over at Anthony.

"Do you smell that?"

"If you mean a strange sweet decaying odor, then yes."

They came to an unexpected rise. As they got to the edge and looked over, their worst fears were again realized. A river twice as wide as the last glistened with a deep red glow like lava. It was beautifully mesmerizing. Unless the lords were masters of creating odors to accompanying their illusions this river was the real thing.

Simultaneously they gasped, "The river of blood."

Thinking of the twins, Anthony realized, "I am beginning to remember that the twins were able to cross this obstacle by using their blowguns as boats. Those must have been some incredible blowguns."

"You don't happen to have anything like that in your backpack?" asked Rosalia.

He was thinking that if they ever got out of this alive, he would write a companion guide to the Popol Vuh.

They both walked to the river's edge.

Rosalia reluctantly knelt down and started to put her finger into the ooze. Anthony grabbed her and pulled her back.

"What are you doing?"

"I thought I would test the waters. You know see, if it really is blood."

"Why don't we find out by putting something besides us in it," Anthony suggested.

Anthony held out a pencil.

"Good idea," reaffirmed Rosalia.

She took the pencil and knelt down, she put the eraser end in about an inch, she was aware of the viscosity as it almost pulled the pencil out of her hand. She immediately pulled it out of the river. The blood hung onto the pencil, and began to slowly run down alive; it was actually pulsating. She realized that it wasn't gravity that was propelling it towards her hand. It seemed alive. They both watched in fascination as blood slowly worked its way along the pencil and then rolled its way over the ground and like a ball bearing to a magnet into the river. It seemed to have a sense of intelligence.

"That's not the blood I had imagined," Anthony remarked.

Worried, Rosalia asked, "If that little drop has those abilities, what can the river do?"

They began to slowly back away. Then after what they thought was a safe distance they began to whisper to each other, not knowing if this newly encountered life form might have the ability to hear them.

Anthony starts off, "O.K. let's go through all our options. You know, let's brainstorm."

"I think swimming is out," smiling while trying to hide her fear.

"I don't even think that if we had a boat, that we would have a chance," Anthony added.

"O.K., let's think about what properties blood has. I remember from my biology class that it is 90% water and then there's the hemoglobin thing," thought Rosalia.

"Where does that leave us?"

"What do you have in your back pack, Anthony?"

"I have a notebook and…"

Rosalia interrupted, "No, no, don't tell me. Empty it out on the ground so we can see."

Anthony began emptying the contents of each compartment into their respective piles.

Rosalia immediately fixated on butane lighter. "That's it," she said pointing at the lighter.

"The lighter?"

"Yes, that's it."

Anthony looked, waiting for an explanation.

"What happens when you heat up a knife and place it on a cut?" asked Rosalia.

"It cauterizes it. Seals it."

"Exactly."

"Are you kidding? We don't have a knife that big," Anthony tried to visualize the process.

Rosalia's expression acknowledged how futile her idea sounded.

Anthony realized that while seemingly ridiculous it was at least an idea, and he had nothing to offer.

He began picking up the small pieces of wood that littered the banks. Placing them into a pile, he took the lighter and lit a fire. It burned quickly. He picked a single piece of wood and walked hesitantly toward the river. As he knelt down he noticed that the river began to flow toward him, he quickly dipped the wood far enough to get a sample.

Rosalia watched as the blood reacted exactly as it did with the pencil, even though the blood was on the end of the stick it was pulsating upward towards Anthony's hand. He quickly held the stick into the fire. What happened seemed like a scene in a science fiction movie. The blood almost jumped off of the stick; however it was too late to react to Anthony. He had already thrown the stick into the fire. Like a pyrotechnic flash, the blood was seared to the stick. The smell was strangely familiar.

Rosalia sighed, "Well at least it can be cauterized."

"Did you see how it almost jumped at me when I knelt down the river? It actually began to flow toward me."

"Are you saying that it could see you?" she asked.

"No, I think that it could smell me."

Rosalia ran over to the contents of the backpack. She pushed everything a side. The concern on her face was alarming to Anthony.

"Where is the COPAL?" she yelled.

"I emptied everything. No, wait. There is that little zipper compartment in the side pocket. Look in there."

Rosalia grabbed the backpack and began to squeeze it. She felt a hard object and found the zipper compartment. She unzipped it and was immediately rewarded by a familiar smell. She grabbed the Copal and held it up as though she had discovered a diamond of similar size.

Anthony was clueless. "This no time for childhood memories."

"No when you said it could smell you, I knew how the twins were able to cross the river. They had brought with them the most sacred thing from their world that they could offer the Lords of Xibalba. It also explains the dead trees next to each of the rivers. All of the sap had been drained from them as offerings. There are no more trees left in Xibalba."

Still confused Anthony asked, "So how does that help us?"

"The locals in Palenque harvest Copal like maple syrup. The lords used all their resources; the only thing left of the forests are these branches scattered along the shore."

Rosalia picked up a large branch. She walked over to Anthony, knelt, down and began untying and then removed his shoelace.

"What are you doing?" demanded Anthony.

Without responding, she then tied the Copal to the end of it. She placed the copal into the fire igniting the tip. Anthony now knew why she was so fond of the smell. But what did that have to do with the river of blood?

Rosalia simply waved to him to follow her. She walked towards the river.

"Remember it can smell you," Anthony reminded her.

She never hesitated as she approached the bank. The Copal was really beginning to smoke, almost as aware of its responsibility as the blood in the river.

She lowered the branch. The river immediately began to retreat, and then in a truly biblical moment it separated. Not since Moses and his staff had any event seemed so epic. It was red and parting to reveal a path of solid ground. Anthony grabbed her hand and walked as fast as he could. As incredible as this was, he didn't want to test what appeared to be a miracle.

"How did you know?" he asked her once they were safely on the other side.

"I didn't. It just seemed to be the only possibility."

"Couldn't we have discussed it before you…?" She stopped him.

"I just knew it was the only decision."

"I understand," he nodded.

As they walked it seemed as though they were in slow motion while the blood was churning against itself creating walls that were constantly advancing and receding. It seemed as though the blood understood they were given safe passage and, at the same time, the need remained wanting to engulf them into the eternal river as so many before them.

CHAPTER 11

The rhythm of the couple's journey was becoming familiar: walk several hours, encounter the impossible, cross the river and on to the next problem. They were both thinking the same thing. How could the next river be nearly as dangerous as the past two? Rosalia was the first to break the silence, since she had been worried about the expected next obstacle the twins had encountered.

"How do you cross a river filled with pus?"

"I know it's not lethal, just disgusting." he said being practical.

"Maybe that's just it." Maybe it's that simple, thought Rosalia.

Their assumptions were confirmed, when they arrived at the next river's edge. It was an eerie white. If you were to order a pigment match at your local paint store, you would probably describe it as similar to a cadaver white with a green/blue tint, and a ghastly glow. This would not be a Martha Stewart color combination. It bubbled and popped, like a teenage face nightmare. The smell was indescribable. Damp and musty, it didn't seem to move, just congealed. Anthony removed his backpack while Rosalia looked on anxiously, thinking he was about to pull an ingenious solution out.

"What is it?"

"What is what?" he reacted.

"What do you have in there that is going to get through this?"

"Nothing. I am just taking it off so I can carry it over my head, I don't want to get any puss on the only supplies we have."

Her expression changed immediately.

Anthony stepped into the goo and began to sludge his way. Each time he pulled his foot out, it sounded like a toilet plunger trying to get out the worst imaginable plumber's encounter. He was now waist deep, however now half way across he realized it wasn't getting any deeper.

"Should I begin to follow you?"

"Not yet. Wait until I get to the other side," he yelled back.

Anthony watched as she went through the same disgusting process.

When they both sat on opposite shore they were both thinking the same thing?

Anthony was first to speak. "What kind of sick bastards would even think up such a disgusting idea?"

Rosalia began laughing hysterically, "Of course everything until now has been a pleasant stroll through the park."

Anthony began laughing and nodded.

CHAPTER 12

The next river was a pleasant surprise. It seemed too good to be real, a silly thought since nothing they had encountered had anything to do with reality.

Rosalia edged cautiously to the river's edge. Antony was still in shock of what he thought he saw, Rosalia gently dipped her cupped hand into the river, and filling it said, "It's water, water."

She raised it towards her nose, smelled it and in one fluid movement put it into her mouth.

"Don't," yelled Anthony.

It was too late. She gulped it down, and then suddenly jerked.

Anthony screamed out, "What is it?"

He felt an incredible pain.

"The biggest ass mosquito bite I have ever seen," quickly responded Rosalia.

A cloud of insects immediately swarmed them.

They seemed the size of hummingbirds. Anthony looked at Rosalia and yelled,

"Say my name."

"Without missing a beat she screamed, "Anthony."

And likewise Anthony screamed out her name.

Almost like a mosquito repellent bomb had exploded, they swarmed off into the distance.

"Now they know our names," said Anthony.

In the Popol Vuh the twins had encountered the mosquitoes and made an ancient pact that if they the insects were to attract the lords they would be given the reward to feed off of the blood of all that entered Xibalba. It was a sweet deal for the twins given that each time one of the lords was bitten. One or another lord would ask them by name what had happened. Were they O.K.? By saying the lords' names the twins had gained a powerful weapon; they entered Xibalba knowing the identity of their adversaries. To the ancient Maya this immediately made them superior, removing the hometown advantage.

CHAPTER 13

Anthony began to panic knowing that their odds weren't in their favor to begin with. He looked at Rosalia who seemed calm and confident.

"Don't worry. I already know the Lord's names," reassured Rosalia. Through her uncle's stories and Mayan pottery images, he had recounted many time the "Lords" and their disgusting features and descriptive names. They were truly the "Four Horsemen of the Apocalypse "times four. There was actually a hierarchy to them. Seven Death and One Death were the original lords. It seems that business was so good in Xibalba that they needed assistants. Their names delighted her the most. Blood Gather, Bone Scepter, Skull Scepter, Demon of Filth, Demon of Woe, Demon of Pus, Demon of Jaundice, and her favorite Demon Scab Scrapper, just the name made her smile. What a ridiculous bunch. As if any of them would allow a scab to develop. They would soon find out that they were all too real.

"That's not the point. You need to be able to recognize each of them individually. Remember there are 12 of them.

"Nobody has that kind of luck," mumbled Anthony aloud.

Rosalia smiled.

"I know who they are," she said. "I think I could pick them out in a line up."

"How is that possible?"

Rosalia gestured to Anthony to come to her and for the first time since they had entered this dark world they both walked into the river and it was cool and refreshing. When they crossed the river they saw something in the distance running fast on all fours towards them. It was impossible to determine the size of this creature since there was nothing to compare its scale to. As though it had gone into warp speed, it was instantly standing in front of them.

"Finally our guide has arrived," smiled Rosalia.

"This is our guide dog? It's a Chihuahua."

His eyes looked like a flash camera photo without the red eye option. He came up to them, smelled their feet. Rosalia extended her hand. Like he had known her forever the dog licked it. She looked at Anthony and then the dog that seemed intently interested in what they were saying. She walked over to Anthony and began whispering into his ear. Even though she was certain that the dog had never heard English before, she wasn't taking any chances he understood, especially given everything that they had encountered seemed to have exceptional abilities. Anthony smiled and nodded.

"Are you sure?" Anthony asked.

"So far every description in the Popol Vuh has been accurate. You will have to trust me. I feel confident."

Anthony put his backpack on. It would be the last time he took it off in Xibalba. The dog turned and began to walk in the direction the swarm of mosquitoes had flown. They walked for hours. The landscape was becoming less desolate compared to their experiences so far, somehow calming. They came upon the occasional bush, tree and then something completely unexpected: a small but well kept field of corn. They walked over to it and Rosalia brushed the silk on one of the ears with her hand. It was real. Could it be that the lords needed the food of the upper world now that their sacrificial blood supply had dried up?

They could begin to see a building in the distance, and then several, becoming larger as they neared a small ridge. The dog stopped, almost anticipating their need to survey their next encounter. It was by no means a city but obviously a well organized complex, much like the ritual centers found in the center of the large urban complexes of most ancient Mayan cities. Missing were the houses of the common Mayan people. If this was

Xibalba there were no common people, only the legendary lords who waited for their prey.

It seemed orderly, each house was raised on a three-tiered platform, and streets divided them into individual compounds. It was by no means main street *Our Town*. But nonetheless it appeared unexpectedly civilized. They could see a ball court on the outskirts.

"I am certain I can do this."

"Wh…?"

"There are 12 houses; that's how many lords there are in the Popol Vuh."

"Do you expect each of to have their names on their mailboxes?" Anthony smiled.

Her expression needed no explanation. She began walking, and the dog was caught off guard, and ran in front of her. Even though they no longer needed his guidance, she allowed him to take charge, somehow anticipating that the lords would be angered at his failure to complete his duties, especially given that it had been so long since he had guided anyone to their death.

As they got closer to the first house, they could see that it had been some time since anyone had visited. The stucco walls were peeling, the paint was barely visible, and it had faded over the centuries. It would seem that the lords had become lazy. Their reputation for vanity in all things they possessed and appearance would become even more evident in a few seconds. She began to study the large stucco relief mask on the roof's gable. Like all Mayan temples it identified to which god the structure was dedicated. The image was easily identifiable as "One Death" with the trace pigment of a singular dot, the symbol of one, still visible.

As she approached the step, a figure appeared from the darkened doorway.

An almost skeletal silhouette emerged; his dress was disheveled and dirty.

This was nothing like she had imagined a lord of the underworld to look like since Mayan kings and gods were depicted in ornate costumes and regalia, richly painted on the walls of palaces and particularly on the thousands of ceramic vessels found in Mayan tombs.

He gestured for her to come up the stairs. Anthony was amazed at how calm Rosalia was. He stood motionless as she began to climb to the upper platform. She immediately bowed and a slight smile came to the withered face of the lord.

He began to speak, but unexpectedly Rosalia interrupted him, startling the lord since he had thought she understood the protocol.

"Good morning Lord Scab Scrapper." Rosalia greeted him by name as she bowed.

Anthony was convinced that they were doomed, given that he was able to identify the house as that of "One Death."

The expression on the lord's face was incredulous.

Lord Scab Scrapper turned to face her, "You know who I am?"

"Your greatness precedes you, not only in your world but in mine," Rosalia explained respectfully.

"Will the *chaneque* be accompany us?" as he glared towards Anthony.

Her expression was of surprise and nodded yes.

Even though she had thrown the Lord off guard when recognizing him by his name, his vanity was now rejuvenated. It had been so long that anybody had praised the Lords of Xibalba. He was impressed by her and perfect dialect. So many of those that had passed before her were common; their dialect was a combination of local tribes and Quiche Mayan, the language of the Kings and most importantly the lords. This strangely dressed person was a welcome relief as long since a visitor to Xibalba.

He asked her to wait while he returned to the interior of his home.

Anthony climbed up the stairs. "How did you know that was "Scab Scrapper" and not "One Death?""

"His eyes were not vacant and large like "One Death" and his skin was peeled back like the images of him painted on the bowls and particularly the hot chocolate mugs so prized by the Mayan kings. When I was little I would draw all of the lords from their descriptions in the Popol Vuh and show them to my uncle. If accurate he would take me to the museum and show me the real thing. It was my reward."

Anthony started to complement her, but she immediately stopped him.

"That's not the incredible thing. He referred to you as a *chaneque*."

Anthony wasn't familiar with that word, and shrugged his shoulders. "A what?"

"A hunchback."

"A what? I'm not a hunchback."

Rosalia smiled and pointed to his backpack. The perfect REI color matched to his Banana Republic outfit made it seamless, His clothes and backpack appeared to be as one to create the appearance to Lord Scab Scrapper of a hunchback. Hunchbacks were mysterious; to the Mayan, they were feared and at the same time revered as semi-divine creatures. Given Anthony's height of 6'2" he was of particular concern to the lord, since most of the Mayan hunchbacks also suffered from dwarfism.

"You can never remove the backpack while we are in Xibalba." commanded Rosalia.

Anthony smiled.

"We have another advantage," said Anthony.

"It would appear so."

Anthony also felt somewhat reassured in Rosalia's statement. "While we are in Xibalba." This indicated to him that there was some hope they would escape the underworld. He didn't mention this to her, in case that wasn't what she had meant after all.

Lord Scab Scrapper reappeared. He had taken his time to put on a fresh tunic, of royal purple, one of the most prized colors of the Mayan Lords, created by dye taken from octopus ink, almost as precious as jade. He had also attended to his hair, reworking the strands into series of plums pushed forward over his forehead. It was, given his initial appearance, a complete makeover. There was still the issue of his skin condition. He gestured for them to follow. The dog took his place as lead and they walked to the next house.

The stucco mask identified it as the palace of the Demon of Jaundice. Lord Scab Scrapper called out his name, and again a figure appeared from the darkened doorway. She looked over to Lord Scab Scrapper and in Quiche said,

"Excuse me Lord we seem to have a visitor."

"What do you mean?" asked Lord Scab Scrapper.

"That is Lord Bloody Teeth," Rosalia quickly reacted.

He looked incredulously at her. She had again identified correctly, even though it was not his house. He knew then that their oldest ploy to humiliate their visitors by failing the most basic etiquette had failed. She approached Lord Bloody Teeth slightly bowed and said, "What a pleasure it is to meet you Lord Bloody Teeth." He was as amazed as Lord Scab Scrapper. He glanced over at him and Scab Scrapper only shrugged his shoulders. The lords seemed confused; their collective egos hadn't been fed in centuries. And now this beautiful unidentified woman had paid them respect and understood the protocol as if she were a princess in a royal court. At the same time they were infuriated. Not since the Hero Twins had anyone successfully identified them.

They took their respective seats in the court's plaza. Each had an elaborately woven mat with a stone stele directly behind it. This time they took their correct positions as identified by the ornately carved reliefs depicting the respective lords. It reminded Anthony of a medieval court. Demon Jaundice was the spokesperson or leader of the terrible twelve. Anthony so wished he could take out his camera for this photo-op, but he would be compromised.

The lords gestured for Rosalia and Anthony to come forward to a gigantic stone slab bench. "Please our honored guests. Take a seat so we can talk. We want to learn all about you."

Rosalia looked at Anthony and cautiously nodded and winked. Anthony replied in kind. She remembered how in the Popol Vuh the Lords attempted to humiliate the twins by having them sit on that very bench, but the twins knew it was a cooking slab, literally a hot seat meant to humiliate them. Like the twins, Rosalia thanked them, but refused saying that it would be inappropriate for them to sit in front of the gods. Again the Lords were flattered and infuriated that their trick had failed. What Rosalia did next was a complete surprise. She pulled her room key out of her pocket, and concealing it in her hand she slowly removed the key, leaving only the Jade plaque.

"We have bought you a gift, and can only hope you will accept it as a tribute to our respect." She handed it to Lord Jaundice. His expression was of shock, having not had one for centuries. No longer did the Mayan surface dwellers make any offerings, let alone Jade. She wasn't worried about them discovering its origins, Taiwan. He passed it around to the other lords. It was obviously a huge success.

What came next was completely unexpected. In unison they spoke and two attendants appeared. They presented themselves to Anthony and Rosalia and gestured for them to follow. They stood up and went up the steps of an adjacent building. There was a simple wood table and two woven cotton mats at either end, the customary sitting arrangement for most Mayan functions. They sat down and crossed their legs. The attendants disappeared through a beautiful red curtain.

"I don't remember this part in the Popol Vuh. Where are all of the challenges?" Anthony asked Rosalia.

"I don't know. Maybe that was only reserved for the twins."

The curtain opened and the two attendants carried a large tray filled with bowls and pots. The smell was overwhelming. This time the odor was a familiar and pleasant one of corn, beans, and squash. And for Rosalia there was a smell of her favorite childhood memory, hot chocolate. Her uncle would always bring her a steaming cup in the morning to her bed and greet her. "Princess Rosalia the drink of Mayan Lords." She had only seen the richly painted 'Chocolate Mugs' in museums. Most had been discovered in burials of Mayan nobility and the wealthy elite. Mayan murals depicted numerous images of chubby figures that had undoubtedly over indulged in their beverage.

They both wondered how such a feast could have been assembled. The only sign of agriculture was the small cornfield they had seen on the entrance into Xibalba yet the rest of the fields were barren. The Lords looked under nourished.

The attendants looked longingly at each of the dishes as they placed the before them. It was obvious that they hadn't seen anything like this for some time. They again disappeared through the red curtain.

"What should we do? Do you think it is poisoned?" Anthony whispered.

Anthony was startled as Rosalia grabbed the chocolate mug and began gulping down the thick sweet froth. She stopped for a moment and finally answered Anthony. "They wouldn't waste this feast, let alone on two potential sacrificial victims."

Her words were bitter sweet, but Anthony joined in. It was a welcome change from the few rationed bites of the power bars and granola that Anthony had stashed in his backpack.

The next thing Lord Jaundice requested was a friendly game of ball.

"While we know some of your customs, we are unfamiliar with the ball game. Since nobody has played it for many years," Rosalia answered.

The Lords looked perplexed and saddened, realizing that the upper world had fallen silent.

'They don't respect us anymore," said Demon Jaundice.

Rosalia shook her head. "No my lords. As you can see, your legend has persisted for many cycles of the long count."

He smiled.

Demon Jaundice challenged, "Then you know it is our custom to challenge our guests to friendly competitions."

Rosalia bowed her head again and nodded, looking out of the corner of her eye at Anthony as he did the same. They both grinned and winked at the same time as the Lords were talking among themselves.

CHAPTER 14

"We would like to test your abilities since you are unable to engage us in our favorite pastime." There seemed a collective relief given that none of them had played the ballgame for centuries. They could still keep the illusion of their prowess alive by not taking the field in the ball court. Nothing was said but understood by them this was their first victory over these strange visitors. At the same time, Rosalia was thinking what a shame not to be able to see these ragged lords in one of the most sacred rituals of life and death. She almost spoke up and challenged them. After all, as a child, she had played with her friends in the ball court at Palenque. What she knew was an intramural version, and these guys, even given their appearance were Varsity in experience.

Demon Jaundice began the challenge. "We would like to have you perform a simple task that involves none of the difficulty of the ballgame."

He held out what appeared to be a cigar.

Rosalia smiled, knowing full well what the test involved. "You would like us to smoke?"

"Yes a friendly challenge, we invite you to go into the "House of Darkness" using only the embers of the cigars to light you way, and to keep them burning until morning."

Rosalia smiled. "You truly are trying to accommodate us. I think we can easily complete your request."

All the lords smiled and then began to laugh.

Rosalia and Anthony knew the story of the twins' challenges, so they felt sure they knew what was coming next. Demon Jaundice's voice was even higher and more annoying unable to hardly contain his glee. "Did I forget to mention that in the morning we want you to emerge from the House of Darkness with your cigars intact? Oh and yes, I forgot to mention that there would be a guard and a watchman who will check to see that they are constantly burning."

Shocked Rosalia replied, "My lords that is impossible. We would have to be magicians or gods."

To which the Lords howled with laughter, since they knew that this task would defeat these strangers.

Again Rosalia played her innocence. "What will happen if we fail?"

"You will be honored by being sacrificed to the Lords of Xibalba."

Again the lords laughed.

Rosalia looked terrified and grabbed Anthony. This was just the response the lords had expected and witnessed so many times in the past. Two figures emerged in the dusk. The guard and the watchman escorted them to the entrance. It lived up to its namesake, a pitch-black interior awaited them, the guard handed them two pieces of flint to light their cigars and then closed the door behind them. They immediately hugged each other.

"We have them where we want them," whispered Rosalia.

Anthony who hadn't spoken in sometime asked, "What do you mean?"

"Don't you remember what the twins did to fool the guard?"

"They used feathers from a Macaw to fool them into thinking they were flames, but we don't have feathers," replied Anthony. He stopped himself." But we have the halogen flash lights; we could stay here for three nights, and they would think that we were magicians keeping the same cigars lit forever."

"I never knew how sexy a hunchback could be," smiled Rosalia.

She turned him around in the darkness." Which pocket are they in?"

"The left bottom zipper."

She removed two-pencil thin flashlights and turned them on, handing one to Anthony. At that moment the door opened a crack and the guard mumbled something and closed the door, obviously satisfied that they were able to ignite their cigars and that he would be having a short night and be able to soon report to the Lords than their cigars had burned out. The Lords would surely reward him. They would have the victims they needed for their long awaited sacrifice. Xibalba would be celebrating tonight.

Anthony surveyed the interior with their light; they realized that they were probably the first to actually see the house since it was in constant darkness. It was cavernous; the floors were dirt and there was a series of ridges in the distance. As they approached, they turned their lights downward. A long ravine ran the entire width with numerous skeletons at the bottom. It would appear that nobody got out alive. They walked back and just as they sat on the floor the door opened again. The same grumble came from the guard as he saw them each holding a brilliantly lit cigar. An almost anticipated rhythm began to get shorter and shorter between the intervals as the guards checked on them. *Certainly their end is near,* thought the watchman. Rosalia and Anthony could hear the two of them outside the door. Rosalia put her ear to the door and could hear them shouting at each other. Anthony asked her what was going on.

She walked back and sat beside him.

"They are afraid. It is almost dawn and we still have our cigars are burning brighter. They are afraid this challenge may be a failure."

What seemed like about 15 minutes went by, then they heard the door begin to open. A crack of daylight penetrated into the room. Then almost as though they had rehearsed, Rosalia and Anthony turned their flashlights off and put them into their pockets. It wasn't the guards this time, but the lords looking in anxiously.

Their expressions turned to anger as both Rosalia and Anthony held out their cigars as pristine as they were when given to them the day before.

The lords were outraged; they attempted to hide their anger by complimenting Rosalia and Anthony. Their tone was as false as the smiles on their faces. They walked back to the plaza and assumed their respective places. Again Rosalia and Anthony refused their offer to sit on the large stone slab.

CHAPTER 15

The lords were deep in conversation. Their gestures were almost pantomimic.

Anthony couldn't help notice the sly smile on Rosalia's face.

Anthony whispered without moving his lips. "What is so amusing? They seem really angry. I think we are in real trouble this time."

"The house of knives is our next challenge," responded Rosalia.

"Why is that something to smile about? The cigars at least weren't dangerous, just the challenge, but knives can kill us."

"Remember the twins," she said.

Anthony immediately remembered how in the Popol Vuh the twins had encountered the same challenge. They were successful in surviving the night by befriending the knives, and in the morning greeting the lords without a scratch.

"So you really think we are going to encounter a room full of razor sharp obsidian blades and have a sit down to get to know us?"

"No," said Rosalia. "I think that like the cigars, there is a trick. They're not actually talking blades, real ones but I think we can figure this one out, too."

As though everyone were reading the same page, the lords summoned them towards them. "We would like to invite you to another friendly challenge since you were so successful with the cigars. This challenge will seem almost insulting, yet humor us," said the lords.

"There is no need to entertain us. Your hospitality is enough," Rosalia responded graciously.

The lords seemed to chuckle. The thought that they were trying to entertain the guests who were naïve enough not to realize that the lords were trying to kill them, made them confident that this would be the last challenge necessary.

"We would like you to spend the evening as our guests in the House of Knives."

Rosalia asked, "So what is the challenge?"

The Lords knew that they had them this time.

"Only to remain the night and be our guests for breakfast in the morning."

"I can only hope that you receive all strangers with such hospitality," replied Rosalia.

The lords smiled and nodded agreeing.

The same guards approached them and gestured for them to follow. They walked past the location of last night's challenge. The door was closed and a wooden latch that hadn't been there when they entered sealed it, as though the lords had realized that that last night was the last time the cigar challenge would ever occur in Xibalba. They walked for several minutes. As they approached the next house, they could make out the fragments of the sculpture on the roof comb. Like most structures in Xibalba, it had been centuries since the surface had been replastered and painted. The lords had really let the place go. There were two doors; the guards opened the door on the right and told them that they would come for them in the morning and meet them at the door on the left.

"Do you understand?" asked the guards. Pointing again at the door on the left. Rosalia and Anthony both nodded and pointed at the left hand door. They were thinking, did they look that stupid? The doors were right next to each other. It wasn't like they could get lost unless some how the interior wasn't anything like the exterior, but even then.

Anthony and Rosalia didn't even hesitate. They walked in and the door shut immediately behind them. However unlike the previous encounter there were two torches attached to the walls. The room was dimly lit, but at least they could see. The interior led into a corbelled passageway; they also noticed that the interior was narrow and the left hand door wasn't in that room. It was clear that they were supposed to enter the passage way in order to get to their prescribed destination in the morning.

Anthony first, "Where are the knives? I want to make as many friends as possible before we do this."

Rosalia began laughing. "Did you think that they would be here to greet us like puppies? I thought you understood what I meant back there."

"I have to tell you nothing is what I imagined it to be like. When I read *Alice's Adventures in Wonderland*, I never expected her to fall down the rabbit's hole and actually experience 'Wonderland.' I'm sorry that I haven't figured this out like you have."

This was the first time during their entire ordeal that they had ever had any rift. Rosalia immediately picked up on Anthony's angst. She quickly responded, "No, no, I am sorry. I didn't mean it that way, I don't have this figured out, but I feel confident that we at least have a road map. We know what is coming next. Remember not everything has been exactly the way it was described. The river of scorpions was an illusion. This could be the same thing."

Anthony interrupted her. "I know, but the River of Pus was not."

"You're right. We need to be cautious. I am taking for granted that the *Popol Vuh* should be taken literally, the way my uncle and the rest of the Quiche do. I always thought that to question it would be like doubting the Old Testament, but then how many would ever have the opportunity to experience Moses and the parting of the Red Sea?"

Anthony smiled and nodded. He took his backpack off for the first time since the cigars. Then took out the halogen flashlights, and handed one to Rosalia.

"Let's check it out," he said.

They walked to the entrance of the passageway.

Anthony began focusing the beam on the floor and then the wall, and eventually to the ceiling. Rosalia watched intently.

"What are you looking for? I don't see anything."

"I am looking for the invisible," he said.

"What?"

"I am looking for the same thing that got us into this mess."

Rosalia looked both confused and concerned. She thought the stress was really getting to him.

"Anthony, are you all right? What do you mean by the invisible?"

All of a sudden Anthony seemed to confirm her fears. He walked into the passage and then knelt. He took the flashlight and focused on a gap between two of the paving stones of the flooring. He motioned for her to join him.

"I thought we were going to be cautious," she said.

Anthony again motioned to her.

She joined him, kneeling next to him. He looked at her and smiled. "What do you see?"

She looked for several moments, and could only see a well-crafted stone floor typical of Mayan craftsmanship. Rosalia shrugged.

Anthony was noticeably pleased with himself. "Look at the edge of the second stone."

She nodded in agreement.

"Notice how meticulous the edges are on the stones. They are exactly level and smooth and then again the nodules appear on each alternating stone. Does it remind you of anything?"

Rosalia immediately understood. "The tomb. Very subtle but obviously intentional and each of those stones is stained a deep red."

"Exactly."

"What do you think it is?" asked Rosalia.

"I can only guess, but given the sophistication of the "glyph button" in the tomb and the mechanism, it could be something equally as ingenious."

"What do you think it would trigger?" wondered Rosalia.

Anthony directed his flashlight several feet in front of the stone, and pointed to several piles of dark shiny debris. "I think those are obsidian fragments," he said.

He then pointed his flashlight along the upper wall close to the ceiling illuminating two perfectly carved diagonal grooves.

"What do you think those were for?" he asked.

"I don't think they are past tense. I think they are still functional. You're going to think this is a stretch, but did you see *The Last Crusade*?"

"You mean Indiana Jones?"

And, at the exact moment, they both yelled. "The penitent man."

"What should we do?" Rosalia asked.

"We need to put weight on one of the stones and see what happens."

Again the backpack came off and Anthony opened the middle compartment. He took out his travel umbrella, extended the handle and looked at Rosalia for approval.

"Are you planning to use that to push on the stone? And if so that is only going to give you a 3' advantage. We don't know how this thing works."

"We do know that those grooves are likely what the blades travel on, and if I am kneeling, I should be a good 2' lower than the path they will take."

"But in the movie it took at least 5 tries before he figured out the right solution."

"Well given that we are only a cast of two, we had better hope that I am right on the first try, or else I will never know what your solution was," Anthony quickly replied.

Anthony handed her the backpack and began to kneel.

"Wait," yelled Rosalia. She removed the rope from the pack and tied it around his waist.

"Just a safety line but, maybe if something goes wrong, I can pull you out of the blade's path."

"I think anything is a good idea, given we are only working on assumptions," he said smiling.

He again knelt down, slowly extending the umbrella towards the first stone and began to prod the nodule on its front edge. Nothing happened. He began to apply more pressure. Still nothing. Then he pushed more until the handle of the umbrella was noticeably bending. He stopped and looked back to Rosalia.

Rosalia guessed, "Maybe those are just aesthetic. I don't know."

Anthony edged forward a little, wondering if he needed to apply more weight.

He repeated the same process to the right hand side. Still nothing. Then to the center, and then the left. Maybe Rosalia was right. He then leaned out even further and began to probe the nodule on the back of the stone. The tip of the umbrella was barely resting on it when a deafening screech echoed through the room, accompanied by a blinding flash of sparks and then a loud shattering crash. Rosalia immediately pulled with all her strength on the rope, and then fell backwards as the loose end of the rope flew overhead. She screamed Anthony's name, still unable to see anything and choking from the smoke.

The guards looked at each other, smiling, knowing that the deadly trap they had set the day before would yield the same grisly results as they had in the past. Surely the lords would be in a celebratory mood and reward them accordingly. Protocol prevented them from notifying the lords immediately, since the challenge officially ended at sun rise, they chuckled thinking how 12 hours would change the outcome for two headless victims.

Back inside Rosalia heard coughing, and then saw Anthony crawling towards her.

"Are you alright?" she asked. He still had the rope tied around his waist, a two-inch length dangled from his side. "What happened?" she asked again.

Finally he was able to speak.

"I don't know. It happened so fast."

The smoke began to settle. The floor was covered with obsidian shards.

"The obsidian fragments must have cut the rope," replied Anthony. At that moment he realized that if he had Rosalia's well-intended tug, it would have pulled him upright and likely decapitated him as intended. Anthony was right, the floor was mined, and the grooves were the guide tracks for the obsidian blades, but what caused the blinding flash?

Rosalia knelt down and picked up a small piece of gray stone, immediately identifying the cause of the flash. "The sacred stone is flint; it would appear that the lords are highly skilled in pyrotechnics. What an excellent diversion blinding the victim," she explained.

"Victim? That was me. It is a little more personal than just the victim."

"O.K. What do we do now?"

"We have to continue, if we are not at the door at sunrise, we have failed even though we survived the impossible challenge."

"Do you think that's it? I mean was that the challenge?" Rosalia asked hopefully.

"Well if this is the House of Knives that was one and there could be more."

"At least we know what to look for," Rosalia said.

"That's assuming that all of the blades are rigged the same way. Given how effective this was, we are lucky to be alive. I doubt that given the deep red floor stain, very few have gotten beyond this point," reasoned Anthony.

He directed his flashlight beyond the first several stones. None of those had any indication of the blood stained surface that was only inches away from the near fatal experience.

"I still think we should assume that each stone has the potential to trigger knives," warned Rosalia.

"You're right."

He untied the rope around his waist and took the rope that Rosalia was still gripping in her hands. He rolled it up and put it back into his backpack. The next several hours were tediously slow, given that they had to crawl and like a bomb squad, they probed each stone expecting the worst. The umbrella was starting to get a pronounced bow to it.

Rosalia took her flashlight to shine on the ceiling. After several moments she stood up.

Anthony grabbed her hand pulling her to the floor. "What are you doing?"

"Look, the grooves stop here. There are no tracks. They really didn't expect anyone to get this far."

Anthony had to agree.

Anthony also noticed that the nodules on the pavement had also disappeared.

"The nodules are also gone, Rosalia."

They both stood up together.

"We still have to be careful," he warned her.

It felt good to be standing. The cramps in their knees began to fade. They walked step by step, each moving their flashlight up and down the walls and the floors looking for anything that would indicate that the lords had thought to anticipate anybody making it beyond this point. They eventually got to the first turn in what had been a long straight path. As they approached the corner, Rosalia grabbed Anthony's hand and stopped.

"We have to assume that this is a trap, not just a turn in our journey. We need to see what is around the bend," warned Rosalia.

Anthony nodded and took a small nylon zippered compartment from his backpack. She was still amazed how organized he was. He opened it and pulled out a compass.

Rosalia asked, "How is knowing the direction we are headed going to help us?"

Anthony didn't respond.

He took the compass and opened the back. The compass swiveled out as the light from her flashlight reflected back blinding her briefly. It was a mirror. Like everything Anthony had it was the ultimate Boy Scout edition. It was a signaling mirror in case you became lost; the reflection could be used to get the attention of rescue teams. She knew that was not his intent but wished that they had that option.

Anthony stood right at the corner of the turn and took the mirror in his left hand and positioned it at a right hand angle pointing around the edge. Holding it up to his eyes, he took his flashlight and carefully began moving it from ceiling to floor and along the walls of their new challenge. There was no indication of the nodules stained floors or any of the wall grooves from their first encounter. In a giant leap of faith Anthony rounded the corner and stood in the passageway. Rosalia screamed. They both waited for the inevitable. Nothing happened.

"I wish you would let me know what you're going to do ahead of time. You are all I have down here. You have to promise me that you will never do that again," she pleaded.

He nodded sheepishly, knowing she was right. There was both a sense of concern and terror in her voice. The good news was as he moved the beam of his flashlight up and down the walls, they both noticed that the walls didn't seem to have any of the ominous grooves and the floor didn't have the signature nodules.

"Maybe that's the end of the ordeal. They didn't expect anyone to get this far," agreed Rosalia. "I think you are right. However, given everything so far the idea that logic would somehow apply to Xibalba hasn't always proven to be true. Let's assume that every step is our first."

Anthony began a slow surveillance pace down the long corridor. Rosalia mimicked his every move and gesture. After several minutes they had made considerable progress with their circumstances. Rosalia was the first to notice the block stone masonry of the walls seemed somehow different. She tugged on Anthony's backpack. He stopped immediately.

"What is it?"

"I'm not sure," she said. "There is something different about the walls. I can't explain."

"I'm not sure I see what you mean. Maybe different workers cut this stone? It looks like the same stone and patterns."

Rosalia nodded. "I guess I am just being overly cautious."

They resumed the slow journey. Rosalia still had the sense that things had changed; something about the shadow pattern that their flashlights cast on the wall was different. Before she could say anything a series of flashes, explosions and the sound of shattering obsidian echoed down the hallway. The smoke from the flint filled the air and obscured the interior. She tried to cry out but could only gasp trying to get enough clean air to maintain. She began walking forward reaching out hoping to touch Anthony. Nothing then she tripped, falling over something and hitting the floor. She felt sharp pains in her hands and knees, and the obsidian was lethal. Bleeding she reached over to Anthony. He seemed lifeless. She began slapping his face and then began CPR. She had only gone through several repetitions of chest then, breath when Anthony began choking.

The smoke had begun to clear and she could now see, his face and chest were covered in blood. Rosalia feared the worst until he opened his eyes and smiled. He looked remarkably well when she then looked down at her hands and realized that the blood was hers.

Anthony sat up and immediately pulled his backpack off. He noticed that the entire outer compartment had been severed and was lying behind him on the floor. The obsidian blades had almost hit their mark but got the backpack instead. That was the force that threw him to the floor; again a stroke of luck had saved him. He pulled out his first aid kit and began cleaning Rosalia's wounds.

"Are you O.K.?" he asked.

She nodded still in shock that Anthony had so quickly been resurrected from what she thought was certain death. He took a large square of cotton gauze and was relived to see that the wounds were really superficial. Like tiny scalpels the obsidian had cut only through the surface of her palms, and a little Neosporin with bandages and her hands and knees were stabilized as her pronounced that the patient would live and make a full recovery.

Anthony said," I know what happened."

Rosalia stopped him from going any further. She realized the same thing,"' I know. The walls were different; it wasn't the pattern; it was the depth of the seams in masonry, but only the vertical joints. That's why the shadows were different. The blades were rigged to follow the channels this time rather than a single diagonal assault. They rigged a barrage, to assure that if anyone had been fortunate enough to make it this far that their demise would soon follow."

As shocked as Rosalia and Anthony were with recent events the guards were completely taken by surprise. The guards usual siesta duty guard duty time waiting was disrupted by a terrifying sound they had never heard before.

One guard asked, "Do you think they are still alive? What was that explosion? The House of Knives has never shaken like that before."

Not knowing how to answer those questions, the second guard said, "We only have an hour before daylight, then we can open the door. If they did make it to the second challenge, I don't see how they could have survived. I am glad we didn't summon the lords earlier. They would have been furious with us."

His friend nodded with a nervous smile.

It seemed a long night to the guards until they saw the dim light of what was considered daylight in Xibalba. They were both relieved and apprehensive.

They positioned themselves at the door to perform the routine ritual of opening the huge stone slab, but then nothing had been routine since these strangers had arrived in Xibalba.

It truly was a monumental effort for the guards to swing the enormous monolith open. As the light began to illuminate the entrance, nothing could have prepared the guards for what they saw. Standing upright and smiling were what had to be two ghosts. They appeared to be real and then the unbelievable happened. They spoke.

Anthony spoke first." Thank you for guarding us. It is both a relief and a pleasure to see you again."

The guards were speechless, they attempted to smile, but could only gesture for the couple to come out. Rosalia took Anthony's hand while he gently cradled her bandages.

The guards began a slow pace towards the lords. They passed a large walled enclosure that seemed the size of a football field. The walls were easily 20' high. Maybe that was the sacred ball court the couple thought. Rosalia whispered to Anthony. He looked up and then stopped. The guards were 50' ahead of them before they noticed. Immediately the guards ran back, angered that their wards hadn't followed, but more at themselves that they couldn't even accomplish a simple task.

One of the guards started walking faster and clearly was headed to the palace on a mission. As they rounded the corner they could see the guard engaged in a what appeared to be an argument with the lords, and then almost in unison they turned toward Rosalia and Anthony. Their anger was clearly noticeable even at this distance. And then in a single motion Lord Jaundices took the guard by his hair and ripped his still beating heart from his chest then held it above his head, shaking it towards Rosalia and Anthony who were clearly shocked by this barbaric act. The other guard dropped to his knees. As the lords approached he held out his obsidian knife. Again Lord Jawndess repeated the act, only this time using the knife instead of his long bloody fingernails. It was obvious that the hospitality they had feigned earlier to Anthony and Rosalia was now in short supply. The lords gestured for them to walk towards the courtyard. No one spoke a word. They took their respective thrones. Lord Jaundess summoned an elaborately dressed priest who held out a stone bowl filled with both hearts. The priest then walked toward the large heated stone slab.

CHAPTER 16

Both Anthony and Rosalia knew what was next. He took out an unlit torch igniting it with the fires that blazed beneath their welcoming bench. He placed the torch into the bowl sizzling the blood and the hearts. Both the sound and the smell was sickening, sweet and intoxicating. As the smoke rose, the lords cheered as their sacred offering was validated. It was obvious to Anthony and Rosalia that given the elaborate ritual preparation, the sacrifice had been planned; however the victims had changed. And in this case blood was blood as long as the gods were appeased.

The lords turned and began walking towards the palace council house, no indication given to Anthony and Rosalia to follow. The twelve disappeared into the dark interior. Two guards closed the doors behind them, and assumed their appropriate places on either side of the entrance. Rosalia and Anthony both looked at each other wondering what they were supposed to do. Rosalia was the first to speak.

"It's all true, *The Blood of the Kings* is real. The exhibition and catalogue *The Blood of the Kings,* was ground breaking; not that I ever questioned the Mayans lust for blood sacrifice, but I wasn't prepared. The images on the pottery the gruesome frescos at Bonampak depicting victims with their fingertips cut off, bleeding to death, all for the amusement of the Mayan lords standing over them is real."

Anthony added, "I know it's disgusting. Somehow when you research and study their culture all of that seems distant and removed."

They were both staring at the lifeless body of the guard lying face down in his own blood. Neither one of them had ever been this close to death. Only minutes ago they were following the guard, and even though they had really never had a true conversation, he had become familiar and in a way a reassuring sight. He was the first thing they saw as they emerged from each of their ordeals. And while he was never happy to see them, he always treated them cordially as he and his companion escorted them back to the lords. And now they were both dead.

"What do you think we should do? Just wait for them?" asked Rosalia.

"It's very strange. They didn't leave guards. Maybe there aren't any more, except for those two guarding the council palace."

Both of them were thinking the same thing. Other than the lords, there weren't any other people in Xibalba. No attendants, servants or workers only the priest and the four guards, now two. That would explain why much of Xibalba was in a state of ruin. It was truly a skeleton crew. The grandeur described in the Popol Vuh was now only decaying stucco and peeling paint. Could it be that over the years the lords had run out of visitors, sacrificial victims and had turned to their own people for the blood necessary to appease and exalt the gods? It would make sense as a last attempt to re-establish their glory and their divine right to rule Xibalba. Like a pumped up regime they had exhausted all the resources including the very essence of their civilization. They seemed to have forgotten one thing, there was no one left to rule over.

Anthony grabbed Rosalia's hand and began walking away from the plaza. He stopped and looked over his shoulder, neither one of the guards moved or seemed interested in them. Anthony seemed to know exactly where he was going. They were headed towards the House of Knives. They turned the corner and were greeted by an old friend, the Chihuahua, lying next to the enormous wall they had walked past several hours earlier. It was almost comical since his size made the wall look even taller. As soon as he saw them he ran towards them. They were excited to see something both familiar and friendly. Rosalia knelt and, like a pet from the past, he sniffed and licked her hands.

Anthony leaned down and whispered in her ear, "We still don't know if he is a dog or a spy."

"The lords'spy dog? He's a dog and the first real thing that we have encountered in this ridiculous place," Rosalia defiantly interrupted.

Anthony began to walk ahead. He seemed somehow both familiar and connected to this strange space. He was particularly fixated on the unusual light that illuminated the upper edges of the wall like a light show reflecting off of the eerie sky of Xibalba that was almost like a ceiling. "I think I know what this is."

He stopped and looked back at Rosalia.

Rosalia walked over to where he was standing, with the dog right by her side.

"What is it?" she asked.

"A *cenote*," he answered with confidence.

"Why would there be a cenote in Xibalba? A sacred water passage? We are already in the underworld."

Mayans designated specific wells and water passages as sacred. They were conduits or portals that the soul would journey, eventually ending in Xibalba. It made no sense to Rosalia that there would be a need for an entrance into the underworld. Why would the lords recreate a feature that was so essential in the upper world? It made sense up there to reinforce the belief in Xibalba and the domain of the lords who resided there. It served as an important reminder to the living of their responsibility to the 12 legends that would control their fate in the next world.

Just as Anthony was about to explain his *cenote* theory, the dog started barking and began walking to the corner of the walled enclosure several yards ahead. He disappeared around the corner, and then reappeared and again vanished. It was obvious to both of them that they were to follow their little canine companion. They turned the corner and about 100 yards away the dog sat looking in their direction and began barking again. He was sitting next to a strange structure adjacent to the large wall. As they got closer they could see that it consisted of a series of ramped levels culminating in a roofed open structure. The dog immediately assumed his place next to Rosalia who again knelt down and began petting him and talking to him.

Rosalia asked, "What is it, what so important about this place?"

Half expecting him to speak, he just wagged his tail and licked her hand. Anthony began walking around the tower and Rosalia followed. She stopped as they rounded the final corner.

"Did you notice the different levels?"

"Of course, I did."

"How many levels were there?" she asked.

"I didn't count them. Do you want me to walk around again and count them?"

"No I already did that."

"And, are you going to tell me?" Anthony wasn't in the mood for a guessing game.

"13. That's exactly the number of stair levels we walked down into Pakal's tomb.

"You mean the number of levels to heaven, according to the *Popol Vuh*?" Anthony asked hoping he understood the connection.

"Precisely," she said.

"Well, if this is a' Stairway to Heaven,' it ends in Xibalba."

"No, I think the early translators of the *Popol Vuh* took the concept of heaven too literally," said Anthony.

"Now that we have experienced Xibalba, I think they meant the upper world, our world, the any place but here world," reasoned Rosalia out loud.

"You mean now that we have experienced Xibalba, you understand what heaven is and you think this is another portal. A way out?"

Just as she was about to answer, the dog began barking. They looked up and couldn't see anything, and then around the corner the two guards appeared.

"I don't feel good about this," Rosalia mumbled. The guards gestured for them to follow, like their counterparts had done before. Without surprise they escorted them to the plaza where the lords were waiting, sitting on their appropriate thrones.

They both knew this would be the last time they would be summoned to the plaza. The next words out of the Lord Jaundice mouth confirmed their fears. They would undertake the final challenge, the House of Bats. His face lit up with the most diabolical smile. He almost choked as he shouted the newest and last challenge. It reminded Anthony of the Iron

Chef, as the challengers were given the secret ingredient to prepare. Anthony and Rosalia knew these weren't just any bats; according to the *Popol Vuh*, the ingredient would be Vampire Bats. Rosalia was more familiar with this variety, since they actually did exist in her world and were mainly content with feeding off of cattle with no known interest in humans. Also they both were aware that this was the most difficult challenge the Twins encountered during their time in Xibalba. This challenge cost one of them his head. They knew that the results would be different if the same fate came to one or both of them. They had none of the magical powers that the twins possessed to re-attach a decapitated head.

There was also something different in the protocol of the last challenge. This time all the Lords stood up in what appeared to be a well rehearsed procession, paired off in pairs. It reminded Rosalia of her doctoral graduation, after her major professor hooded her with the coveted symbol of the doctorial degree. After all her peers went through the same ritual, the music began and the professors walked in step down an aisle and the newly anointed followed them out of the auditorium. They both wondered why this time the usual guard escort wasn't enough. The Lords seemed even more full of themselves, again reminding her of pompous attitude most of the professors assumed as soon as donned their doctorial robes.

Anthony and Rosalia, without asking, began walking behind the twelve.

They passed by what were now familiar sites—the House of Knives, the Houses of the Lord. Then they turned down a wide avenue that they had not yet encountered. They marched for what seemed almost a mile. There was an abrupt end to this grand thoroughfare. Dead-ending into the side of a small hill, one of the few topographical features they had not seen since they arrived in Xibalba. There was an elaborate temple façade built directly in the side of the hill. Usually temples were elevated by tiered platform in descending size to symbolically represent a sacred mountain, with an enclosed interior comprised of three corbel-vaulted rooms. As unusual as this was, the feature that stood out most of all like a neon sign was the freshly painted and refurbished exterior. Unlike all of the other structures in Xibalba that were in marked deterioration, the enormous stucco roof mask and architectural features were painted in bright red, green, yellow and blue pigments. The only other Mayan structure preserved in this condition ever discovered was found at Copan where in the 1980s archeologists discovered a beautifully preserved temple encapsulated in the foundation of a newer temple. Almost as though it had been mummified, its pigments were preserved intact without being exposed for over 900 years. Rosalia had visited it several times; it held special interest to her since the name archeologists had assigned to it was 'Rosalia.' It didn't matter to her how arbitrary the process archeologists used in naming their discoveries. It was significant to her that the bizarrely exaggerated face of a bat stared down at them. Typical were the bulging eyes in a brilliant cobalt blue, face a deep blood red and the plumed headdress an exceptional jade green with yellow tips. It was spectacular! Anthony wished as he had several other times, that he could use his camera.

Everything about this temple was different, not just the apparent recent paint job, but the steps and door were carefully maintained. Why, of all the buildings, was this one kept pristine? Was it to intimidate? That was unlikely given that there were so few people left to do the necessary maintenance. It would appear for whatever reason, this temple still held a significantly active role in the life of Xibalba. As beautiful and impressive as this, it didn't help either Anthony or Rosalia's feelings of what was about to come.

A high impedance screech deafened them briefly. The lords even seemed startled. The door swung open. A figure slowly passed through the opening. It was a man dressed in a pristine white cotton tunic, his hair was braided in the classic Mayan top knotted feathered plume, his ears adorned with jade ear spools and a beautifully crafted jade pectoral. The pectoral was an intricate jade mosaic mask of the bat god. He was stunningly elegant. He made the lords look pedestrian by comparison. But what really stood out were the goggles he was wearing. They were both cool and ridiculous, their shape emulated the bulging eyes of the façade mask, the lenses almost obsidian black. What was he hiding? Was he some sort of hybrid human and bat?

As impressive as he was, it was obvious who was in charge. He bowed to their knee level and spoke without raising his head. Lord Jaundice ordered him to stand. Anthony and Rosalia were standing several stairs behind the lords; they had to crane their necks in order to get a view of what was happening. Jaundice exchanged pleasantries and then without any attempt to conceal his conversation, he gave the priest his instructions. Unlike the previous challenges where Anthony and Rosalia were dropped at the doorstep and left to discover the peril that awaited them, Jaundice graphically laid out their fate to the priest. It was chilling. Even though they knew what the twins had encountered in the House of Bats, they at least had a fighting chance. Jaundice made the priest repeat his instruction. Like a school child it was lesson in rote memory. It was obvious that the priest found the whole exercise demeaning. It was also obvious that the lords wanted nothing to go wrong.

The Priest repeated, "I will give them each a torch. I will give them a map of the caves. I will show them where the Cavern of Bats is located. If they survive the night, their reward is not freedom, but the honor of sacrifice."

Lord Scab Scrapper handed the priest two incense braziers and instructed the priest to place their sacrificial victims hearts into them and ignite them, then place the braziers outside the temple door at daylight. The sacred smoke and the pungent aroma would please both the lords and the gods. Finally the Lords' ordeal would be over and they would be rid of their persistent visitors. Life in Xibalba was about to resume to normal, if there was such a thing.

The Lords turned in the same procession that they ascended the stairs. They departed without even a glance or acknowledgement of Anthony or Rosalia. It was apparent that the couple was already presumed dead.

The priest gestured for them to come towards them. He pointed to the interior, and like condemned prisoners they walked to their fate. Once inside the priest closed the door with the same deafening screech at the closing as when the door was opened. Both Anthony and Rosalia thought it was the enormous door that was emitting the un-nerving sound; however, once they were inside, the intensity and frequency of the screeching was overwhelming. The priest clapped his hands, and in a split second the sounds stopped. It was impressive and frightening to Anthony and Rosalia given that they were told their fate. The bats were both well-trained, obedient, vampires.

Anthony knew that this not the time to tell Rosalia that he was deathly afraid of bats. When he was 11years old he and two friends climbed up into a cliff dwelling in Mancos, Colorado. They were exploring the ruins of an Ancestral Puebloan site that was on his parents' property. Even though he had lived there all his life, there were still places on the ranch that he had never been. He and his friends had noticed this site several weeks prior. The location required a difficult climb so they planned on how to make the assault on the cliff face. They had gathered every piece of rock climbing gear that their friends and parents owned, never telling them of the expedition. Anthony asked his parents if he could have a "tent over" in the backyard with his friends, and his parents unwittingly agreed.

Anthony had set his watch alarm for 5:00am so they could get an early start. Their backpacks were packed with the essentials, peanut butter and jelly sandwiches and, of course, the equipment. It would be a 2-hour hike full of anticipation. The sun was just coming up over the mesa providing a spectacular sunrise. Anthony took the lead since he had more experience than his friends and was adept at finding the best route up the cliff.

This would be a difficult, but not a technical accent if everything went well. He knew that the original inhabitants were able to use the natural topographic features as their route up and down. In some cases where the terrain was exceptionally difficult, they would carve toe and hand holes to create a natural ladder. He stared at the rocks for several minutes, and without saying a word began climbing. At first it was a process of following the sandstone ledges and then the first true obstacle faced him, a sheer rock face. He walked around inspecting surface and then looked over to the ledge that was separated by rock. Just below the edge of the ledge he was standing, he noticed some thing he had never seen before—a series of horizontal toe and hand holes. He thought this was really ingenious, given that it was hidden by the natural sight line. He sat on the ledge placed his left hand in the first hole and lowered his right foot into the next sequence, repeating the process he arrived safely on the ledge. He yelled to his friends to follow. The rest of the climb was uneventful. When he got to the base of the cliff's floor, he couldn't see into the cave area so he pulled himself up. At first he was disappointed, the spectacular cliff dwelling that he and his friends had fantasized wasn't there; it was only a dark cavern.

He took his flashlight out and began walking into the darkness. As his eyes began to adjust he saw the familiar masonry that was the classical signature of Pueblo III Ancestral Puebloan building. As he moved his flashlight along the wall, it seemed endless. Anthony was sure that he was the first person to see this since it was abandoned in the fourteenth century. He had made a real discovery. Then he saw what had to confirm his suspicions. There was a wooden plank blocking the door. If archeologists or pothunters had been there before that door would have been removed. He could hear his friends yelling in the distance, but wanting to secure his find, he grabbed the door without answering them, He would be the first person in 700 years to view the room, but as he removed the door he was startled by a high impedance sound. He was knocked to the ground by an unknown force. He could feel what felt like thousands of claws piercing his shirt and pants. He swatted his face and opened his eyes to see he was covered in bats and there was an endless swarm exiting the door. He completely panicked and began running toward the cliff. And as his friends later told him, he dove into the air falling fifty feet and landing in a pinion pine tree. They were sure that he was dead. It took them an hour to get to him and pull him free from the tree. His entire body was covered in blood and bat guano. Later, in the hospital, his friends kidded him and laughed, but he never saw the humor, nor did his parents. Even to this day when he returns home, he never entertains the idea of returning to the scene and establishing claim to what he still expected would be an important discovery/experience. Now in Xibalba he could only imagine that whatever they were about to encounter in the bat cave would make his earlier encounter pale by comparison.

As he was instructed, the priest handed them each a torch and then the map. This seemed bizarre given that their fate was sealed. Why not just escort them to the bat cave? Why make them go through all the motions? This was truly a sadistic pleasure for the lords and the priest.

They looked at the map and Rosalia turned it to orient it to the shape of the room they were standing in. She grabbed his hand and began walking. They heard a loud clap and screeching began. After they were out of sight of the priest, they stopped and for the first time in what had seemed days they were able to talk. Anthony was the first to speak, he put his lips to her ear and she hugged him. He had to almost shout the noise was so deafening.

"We need a plan more than ever. We just can't follow the inevitable. I so wish we were back in the house of knives."

They knew there was danger but were clueless, that there were knives was a given, but at least they had a chance. "I feel like we are condemned and we haven't even had our last meal," Anthony continued.

At that point he realized that this was not a plan or speech that Rosalia needed to hear. He could feel her body trembling and, though he couldn't hear her, he knew she was crying.

"O.K. I think I know what we need to do," he said.

His voice seemed somehow more confident, even though not completely convincing.

Rosalia nodded waiting for him to speak, "We need to get to the 'bat cave' as soon as possible."

They both began to laugh. It was a Robin and Batman classic moment. All the elements were there—the immediacy, the danger and most importantly the cave. This moment was short lived.

Rosalia responded, "Why the rush? We know what is going to happen. At least we are safe out here."

Anthony noted something that she didn't see. "I don't know if you have noticed that our torches would appear to be burning extremely fast. Since the priest first lit them, they have burned almost a third of the way down."

"But we still have the night vision goggles and the halogen flashlight. What's the problem?" she asks.

"Do you want the good news first or the bad?" he replied.

"You tell me."

"Well, you wouldn't have noticed but the low battery indicator light was blinking in the upper right of your vision screen. I checked yours after mine started to blink."

I am guessing we have 20 minutes left."

"O.K. What is the good news?"

"I'm not finished with the bad news. My halogen batteries died in the House of Knives; yours is probably close."

"Please, what is the good news? Tell me," she pleaded.

"We still have the torches and we know where we are going, The sooner we get there we can see what we are up against before they burn out. We will have to use the goggles and lamp sparingly."

Rosalia grabbed his hand, they walked for several minutes and then came to a crossroads where the tunnel split into three entrances, this would have been a problem initially but the map clearly indicated that they were to proceed through the middle entrance. They looked at each other. It was evident what they were thinking, and at the same instant they walked the middle path. Why would the lords trick them now when they were already assured their victims would soon be offerings to the gods?

In seconds they arrived at what the map indicated was the portal to the cave. By now the torches were only a quarter of their original sizes. It was a cavernous space; the cave ceiling and floor were covered with stalactites' and stalagmites. It would have been spectacular given any other circumstances. In the center was a large irregular rock approximately 15' high. The good news was the screeching was only in the distance and, for now, there weren't any bats.

Rosalia quickly thought aloud, "We need to memorize as much of this as we can. How many stalags are on either side of the rock? How far apart anything that will give us a reference point in the dark? You take right side."

Anthony walked over to her. "Let's agree on what we are going to measure distance by, our unit of measurement."

He took a large step, and then gestured for her to do the same, she strained but was able to match his stride.

"O.K. We will use this as the measurement. Let's walk off how many steps between as many features as we can remember. Use the rock as our reference point. Try to make it as much of virtual experience as possible, and please don't count out loud."

They both began the process, he on the right and she on the left. If the priest could watch, it would have appeared as some sort of strange ritual dance. Rosalia's torch began to flicker. She didn't even look up to see how much time she had left, her pace quickened as now she had completed three quarters of her assignment. Then the room darkened with only Anthony's torch lit. It looked more like a strobe, providing only intermittent flashes. They started to run towards each other, and suddenly it went black. At that very moment the screeching began, only this time it seemed to be moving in waves above their heads. They tried to call out, but their cries were deafened by each new swarm of bats.

Rosalia was the first to begin the process. She tried to calm herself as she reached out. Her hand felt the first marker, a stalagmite with a huge nodule protruding from the middle. She stopped and tried to orient herself, she began to recite a childhood poem. It was the mnemonic device she had used to remember the sequence/layout of labyrinth of monoliths that sprang from the cave floor.

She immediately turned to her right took 3 measured steps and then extended her left arm out. Bingo! Contact. As she silently recited the poem, she had another connection to her childhood. It was like swinging on a jungle gym when once you knew the rhythm you could swing through the air with your eyes closed. Of course, the jungle gym was in a straight line. Her path was at best a zigzag. And then like she had practiced; it was over as she felt the mass of the rock. Now she only had to find Anthony. She began to navigate around the irregular surface, and after several minutes she had come full circle. No Anthony. Where could he be? Could the bats have already taken their first victim? She literally slapped herself for thinking defeat was an option.

In a silent conversation she tried to restore a sense of calm, "I will wait for several minutes, then walk around the rock. If he isn't there, I will use my night vision goggles. I know I agreed to use them only in an emergency and Anthony would certainly approve of this as an emergency.

The screeching sound didn't seem as loud. Maybe her ears had become more accustomed to it. What she heard next made the screeching seem welcomed. It was a loud swooshing noise, like giant wings whizzed overhead, accompanied by a breeze. If that was a bat, it was enormous. She dropped to her knees, strapped on her goggles. The low battery indicator was flashing. It seemed ironic that a light was the warning that the battery was wearing out as it took the little battery power that was left.

She stopped herself when she realized this was no time for Monty Python reasoning. She looked up. The screeching sounds seemed to be circling around the cave, and then silence followed by a series of fast chirps. She remembered her uncle explaining how the bats located their prey. Like sonar blips, they used their bleeps to bounce off of the intended victims, alerting them to the precise distance and location.

In a flash she saw an enormous pair of wings headed directly at her, falling to her stomach, she rolled onto her back, Rosalia could only guess its size as it whizzed over her. The body seemed almost human in proportion, maybe six feet, with a wingspan about the same, the screeching got louder. No more intermittent chatter, and that somehow made her feel safe, at least for now.

She needed to find Anthony. She scanned the cave area where she had last seen him. Walking towards a large stalagmite, she hugged it trying to blend into the typography of the cave in case there was another feeding behavior. She pulled herself around the tower when she could see the next shape in the distance. It wasn't a stalagmite, much too small, like a...it was Anthony! She ran to him. He was huddled in a fetal position, shaking uncontrollably. As disturbing as this sight was to her, she was happy to see that he was alive. She didn't try to talk to him; she hugged him and then stood up pulling him to his feet. At that moment her goggles went black. She knew that there wasn't time to get Anthony calmed and focused enough to get into his backpack to find his goggles. Whatever he had encountered had completely traumatized him. Besides she knew the way back. It was relatively simple unless, of course, the bat activity changed. She pulled him along, returning to the large tower, rotating around and then taking the 12 measured steps she reached out. Where was the rock? Did she miscalculate? She inched forward and as she stretched her arm out her hand felt a sharp pain. It was the rock. She pushed Anthony to the ground and joined him, leaning against the rock. She pulled her halogen light out. Rosalia had resisted using it earlier just in case it would act as a beacon, attracting the enemy. But she needed a quick assessment of Anthony and their surroundings.

She gasped looking at Anthony's face covered in blood, streaming from his forehead. He had a long cut over his right eye. She took her bandana from her neck, pressing it against the wound. She turned the light off and for the first time spoke to him.

"What happened? Are you all right? Please speak to me."

It took several moments for him to respond.

"When my torch went out, I started to make my way back, and then the sound a series of quick high impedance chatters and then a swooshing noise and something knocked me to the ground. If it was a bat, we are in for real trouble. No one will need to sacrifice us, I never told you about my fear of bats, I thought I had it under control, but that changed everything, I freaked."

"I need you here," she demanded. "Whatever it is, you need to get over it. Do you hear me?"

He nodded.

"We need to find a spot that gives us some more protection. I noticed when I was looking for you that there were several areas on the rocks' surface that had slight indentations. That it might help us blend into the terrain."

"You mean a stealth approach to their sonar?"

"Exactly."

They began edging their way around the perimeter of the rock. Then screeching began circling around the cave. They could tell the bats' orbits were tightening closer to the center when the chatter sequence began. Hurriedly Rosalia's hand found the depressions in the rock that they had been seeking. As they leaned into the rock hoping to morph into the terrain, they heard the swooping sound, and then the Rosalia felt something graze against her chest and then the gust of wind.

Anthony was worried. "It knows where we are. I didn't think bats could see, only detect sound waves."

Stating the obvious, Rosalia said," This doesn't appear to be your average bat. We need to see what we are up against, obviously the halogens are out of the question; we need to use your night vision goggles."

The screeching resumed in the distance exactly as it had before indicating that the bats were creatures of habit.

Anthony wondered and asked, "Why do they wait between their attacks. Why not just come and get us? It's obvious they know where we are. When I was lying there after I was knocked down, I was certain that I was toast. I waited for them to descend on me, but they flew away just like now. Are they just playing with us?"

"You're right. This really doesn't make sense. I have been wondering since we entered the temple what if these are vampire bats? What do they feed on? It's obvious we are the only visitors." She corrected herself, "…victims to have entered Xibalba in centuries. It's not like they have a population of willing blood donors to feed these monsters and there aren't any animals, well except our little canine friend and, if that were the case, he would have been gone a long time ago."

"You're right. Something isn't making sense," Anthony agreed.

They both began laughing at such an understatement-like anything had been right since the sarcophagus opened their nightmare.

Anthony took his backpack off. It felt good not to have it a part of him.

He could feel the goggles in his backpack. He removed them and put them on.

"What are you doing?" asked Rosalia.

"I have the goggles on."

"Do they work?"

"I don't think I should take a chance. What if just by checking I use up what little battery left?"

Rosalia thought back to her indicator light moment.

"You're right."

Just as Anthony was about to speak the all too familiar routine began again: first the screeching, then the circling sequence followed by the chattering.

Rosalia grabbed his arm. They both knew they had to find out what they were up against.

Then the swooshing sound, Anthony's hand was positioned on the switch, and in a moment his eyes captured an image unbelievable as the enormous creature whizzed by.

Like before, the sounds quickly became distant. The attack was over for now.

"Did you see them? What are they? Do we have a chance?" she asked anxiously.

"You are not going to believe it."

"It's that bad?" she asked.

Anthony voice was both excited and somehow joyous.

"It's not a them. It's a him."

"What do you mean by a him? A male bat?"

"No a male priest. I think it's our guy."

"You're right you have freaked out. You're not making any sense."

"I think it's the priest; he is dressed in full bat gear, with wings prosthetic arms, talons and a face only a mother bat could love. It happened so fast but I somehow mentally downloaded the image. I can see him clearly in my mind. He reached out towards my head, his claws like blades, and he didn't expect me to duck. His face looked half human and better than anything depicted in the costumes of the priests in the frescos at Bonampak. I always thought that the mural depictions of the Bonampak crawfish costumes would have won any Mardi Gras contest. Wow!"

"But how is he able to fly?" Rosalia wanted him to know.

"This part is a little fuzzy. I think I saw some sort of harness, literally like an elaborate trapeze hookup."

Rosalia was still doubtful. "If it is the priest, how is he able to see us in the dark? He knows exactly where we are."

"That would appear to be true, however the circling pattern would also indicate that there is a set sequence to his flight pattern. But how does he see us? Or does he?" asked Rosalia.

"Remember what was covering his eyes? I think I know what they were."

"Bat goggles right?" answered Anthony.

"Well in a sense you're right, they were to protect his eyes from the light of Xibalba. We think it is low, but for someone who seems to spend his life in the dark, Xibalba could be blinding." Anthony interrupted her, obviously wanting to contribute something.

"To keep his eyes accustomed to the darkness, he has become light sensitive. Years of cave dwelling forced him to develop night vision at the expense of his Xibalba vision."

"Exactly. Do you remember how he looked away when he handed us the lit torches?" remembered Rosalia.

"Yes, this is good."

"Now I'm not following you. We have someone, something flying around us with razor sharp claws, super night vision and yet have two halogen lights and a night vision goggle with maybe one minute of battery left. If we turn the lights on, he will see us immediately. Remember he can see in no light, let alone low light."

"When is a light not a light?" Anthony queried.

"Now you are the "Riddler. This bat thing is really starting to get to you."

"No, you are going to love this. What if we use the halogens to illuminate him? I mean confuse him when we flash the lights directly into his eyes."

"How are we going to do that? He is flying over us in the dark. We can't even see him. If we turn the light on him, he will see us. We need to surprise him."

He knew she was right. Anthony took several moments to respond.

"I think I have a plan."

"Please no more Riddler solutions," said Rosalia.

"This will work. What if I climb up on the rock and find a hiding place. When we hear the circling routine, as he gets close to us, I will use the night vision to determine when we flash."

"What do you mean flash?" asks Rosalia.

"We both turn on our lights, point them up in hope he is blinded by the light."

"He will only wait until his eyes get accustomed to the darkness and our batteries will wear out eventually."

"Oh I forgot an important part. I'm going to jump on his back as he flies by."

"You are going to what? How are you going to? Wait never mind. You forgot he can see in the dark. He is going to see that you are not with me and, he will know that something is wrong," explained Rosalia poking a hole in his plan.

"I have thought of that. We will use my back pack and hat and kind of create a…."

They were beginning to complete each other's sentences and thoughts.

"A mini you?" Rosalia completed his sentence.

"Exactly."

"Ok, once you are on his back, what then?"

"That's the part I'm not sure about. But if I am right about the harness, I should be able to overpower him since he is strapped in. I'll just wait until the ride is over and tie him up."

As weird as this seemed, Rosalia liked his idea. If everything went as planned they had a chance.

Anthony took his hat off. Rosalia could feel something pushing into her side. It was Anthony's hat, followed by his backpack.

"I think if you sit against the rock and cradle the backpack with my hat on top it will look like we are cradling each other and that should look as natural as anything could in here," Anthony reassured her.

Anthony took the vision goggles and halogen, as he reached out and felt Rosalia doing the same thing. They hugged for several moments without saying a thing.

Then Anthony said, "I will make a short whistle when it is time to flash your light."

"How am I going to hear you with the screeching?" she asked.

Anthony emitted a deafening shrill.

Rosalia was not only impressed, but now she knew exactly his whistling technique. She had always been jealous of her uncle when he would put two fingers to his mouth and seemingly break the sound barrier. As much as she tried she could never come close to that sound nor the volume.

"I am going to start my way up the rock. If I have estimated correctly, given the frequency of his last two flights, then we have about ten minutes."

"I will wait for your whistle," confirmed Rosalia.

It took Anthony several minutes before he could find a ledge. He pulled himself up and began feeling for anything that he could hold until he found a series of outcroppings that seemed almost too good to be true. He was making steady progress until he realized he had reached a blunt pinnacle on the top that felt approximately six feet in diameter, judging how far his arms could encompass. This was good news since it would be something to hide behind and, most importantly, a surface from which to jump off if necessary. Just as he began to try to familiarize himself more with his new surroundings, he heard the sound. This time it was very different with acoustics completely changed. He accounted for the difference being on the ground and now almost on the ceiling. He could hear multiple levels of sound, yet the screeching was still dominant, and now he could hear something was strangely reassuring. It reminded him of the first roller coaster ride he had ever experienced. While the ride was both exhilarating and frightening, it was the sound of the wooden tracks and creaking structural supports that made the ride memorable.

This confirmed the priest was using some sort of track system to create his nocturnal fright flight. He could only imagine how terrified all those before him were who had experienced these sounds and died in this cave without knowing what was really happening.

The circling of the priest bat had begun. Anthony put on his goggles and took out his light. It seemed easier. The echoing that he had experienced on the cave's floor had given way to amazing clarity. The priest had made two complete circles; Anthony knew based on the past experiences that the next circle would be the last. He waited until he could hear the creaking sound coming towards him, and then felt the rock begin to vibrate. He turned on the night vision goggles and he was right; the priest was in a completely prone position with huge wings and large talons though not wearing the cool shades. He had adapted to the dark as they suspected. He put his fingers to his lips and whistled and then his goggles went blank. He turned his light on and then in a giant leap of faith he jumped.

Rosalia heard a loud crash. Then complete silence. No screeching, nothing. She cried out to Anthony. There was no response. She could see a light in the distance that seemed suspended about ten feet above the cave's floor. Without thinking she began walking towards it. She called out again, and this time she heard a muffled sound. She began running and she could see a stalagmite. The light was coming from the top, and then her worst fear was realized when she saw blood running down the surface. She screamed his name, "Anthony?"

She heard her name. Anthony was gasping. He flashed his light down and for the first time since they had been in darkness, he saw her face.

Rosalia saw the source of the blood to be their host impaled on the spire. It seemed Anthony hadn't taken into consideration the added weight, even given the ingenious engineering, the lords and time hadn't anticipated an extra passenger.

"Please come down, and be careful. The surface is slippery," she pleaded.

"Wait a minute. I still have to do something," Anthony said.

"What? Just come down," insisted Rosalia. She wanted him safely on the floor.

She could see Anthony trying to lift the body of the priest upward, but he couldn't get leverage.

"Rosalia, I need you to climb up here."

"Why? He's dead. Why do we need him? We need to try and find a way out of here."

"He is our way out of here. Please just do as I ask you," he insisted.

It was about seven feet to where the priest's body rested on the spire's peak. She worked her way up and could see that it must have been a quick death as he had an enormous hole in his chest.

"What do you want me to do?" she asked anxiously.

"Just push him up until I can get a hold of him."

Still confused she asked, "Why are we doing this?"

"We need his heart."

Rosalia immediately understood what he meant.

She began pushing as Anthony pulled. They could hear the suction sound that his body cavity made as they broke the blood seal with the rock. It was disgusting.

Anthony repositioned himself, and climbed over the body while lifting. With one unified lift, the body was dislodged. It tumbled to the cave floor.

They both climbed down and held each other for a brief moment.

"What do we do after we take his heart. The lords are expecting him to hand over ours."

"I haven't figured everything out, but it's a start."

It was uncanny how well they complemented each other. Almost instantly Rosalia responded. "I don't think you have realized how much we need him. Yes, we need his heart, but I also think we need his arms."

"I am not following you."

Rosalia explained, "The lords are expecting him to hand them two smoking braziers with hearts included. They know he is light sensitive. What if in a sign of humility when the lords knocked on the door, he simply opened it and held out the braziers?"

"Wow! I like it, but we still have a problem. We only have one heart. You're not suggesting…"

"Yes I am," said Rosalia

"What?"

"Your copal. You still have it, don't you? Please say you do," Rosalia sounded desperate.

"I almost threw it out the second day. I thought it was silly to be hauling around a one pound blob of sap. I guess I never got around to throwing it away."

"Thank god," she sighed.

"Do you really think it will work?"

He knew her answer before she spoke.

"What do we have to lose?"

The next half hour was at best, unpleasant. What would have been the most disgusting process was amazingly easy. The priest's heart was actually visible thanks to the stalagmite that acted as an enormous obsidian knife, not exactly a scalpel, but definitely acceptable. It was the dismemberment process that was. The only cutting tool that they had was Anthony's well-equipped Swiss knife. All it lacked was a bone saw option. Anthony removed the prosthetic claw from his right hand, and Rosalia did the same to his left. Without saying a word they began removing their host's respective arms. They both knew enough to begin at the shoulder, and take advantage of the joint to get the full extension of the arms. This would be essential to convince the lords.

They knew that if this didn't work there were still three more challenges: The Hot House filled with ragging fires, The Cold House with sub freezing cold and relentless hail and they would be an easy food source in the House of Jaguars.

Once they had finished the surgery, Anthony took his knife out and cut a large section from the leather wings. It was a shame to destroy such beautifully crafted scalloped details and designs. It was overkill workmanship considering the victims could never have appreciated the craftsmanship. He took each of the arms and wrapped the arms and the heart into neat bundles. Rosalia picked up the talons and, without asking Anthony decided to leave the blood on them. She thought it would be an authentic touch for the lords would expect.

They retraced their way back to the main entrance. Both their lights were dimming. Anthony walked to the door and noticed that there were several torches and maps on a rock shelf, a victims' welcome starter kits. He lit two and handed one to Rosalia. She was the first to see the braziers next to the door. She began laughing.

"What could possibly be funny?" he asked.

"It reminds me of that Christmas poem, you know the one where their stockings were hung by the fire place with care in the hopes that Saint Nicolas would soon be there. Well here are the braziers laid out with care in hopes that our hearts would soon be there."

He couldn't help but laugh at the irony.

"Enough of this. We need to practice."

"Practice what?" she wanted to know." We've got a plan."

"The big hand off has to be perfect," Anthony reminded her.

He took the two bundles containing the arms and unwrapped them. After looking at both of them, he handed Rosalia the left arm.

"Why did you give me the left, if anything you should have given me the right one that's the one I cut off."

"This will be more natural," he said.

"What do you mean?"

"You're left handed, and it just seems logical since you know the way you move it."

Rosalia nodded. As weird as it seemed, it was logical.

They both strapped the talons on their respective hands.

The next few minutes would have made an incredible video. Anthony placed the heart in one and the copal the other. It was difficult to hold the braziers. They kept falling due to original owner's new limp wrist syndrome. They realized they had two problems. The elbow and the wrist needed to be moved in a unified gesture. The only solution was to tie the upper arms to their own forearms. That allowed them to manipulate the wrist. It meant that one of them had to stand in front of the other so the lengths of the arms were equal distance. After several attempts, they were working on an armature marionette level. It would have to do.

Rosalia noticed that a dim light began to shine in the crack in the doorsill. Morning in Xibala was almost here. "I think we should light the offering now since the lords will expect the scent. They could already be out there waiting for the signal."

"Wait a minute," stopped Anthony. "What if they speak? They are going to expect to hear a male priest and you know my Quiche Maya wouldn't even allow me to order a hamburger at McDonalds."

"You're right. I will have to stand behind you so I can whisper into your ear, we will have to make it work."

In an instant they had switched their victims arms to facilitate the new choreography. Anthony took his torch and lit the copal first it took several moments to ignite. Rosalia's description was right. It was a sweet pungent smell that given any other circumstances would have been pleasurable except the odor also reminded him of the hearts sacrificed only a day before. Copal truly was the scent of the gods mirroring its human counterparts.

As if on cue there was a loud thud at the door.

Anthony put on the priest's goggles. "Showtime," whispered Anthony.

They each picked up their respective braziers.

Anthony began shoving the door with his right arm and Rosalia assisted with her right. It was difficult to set into motion since they didn't want it to swing wide open, just enough to extend their grisly tribute to the lords. The smoke immediately was sucked out the slightly opened door. They could hear the lords. Anthony and Rosalia expected the Lords wouldn't send the only remaining guard to pick up the valuable cargo.

They both recognized Scab Scrapper's voice as he declared to his consorts that victory was theirs. A sudden chorus of chanting began, "Kulachan, Kulakcan Kulachan, Kulakcan Kulachan, Kulakcan," the Mayan name for Quetzalcoatl, the great feathered serpent god. This must have been the god to whom the Lords had promised the sacrifice, in an attempt to win favor and ultimately improve the dismal Xibalba conditions. Lord Scab Scrapper demanded, "Come, Pitan, give us our prize."

Anthony's body began to shake. Rosalia rubbed his side with her free hand and began to whisper in his ear Quiche, slowly and with almost phonetic exaggeration Pitan's Quiche response.

"My lords, I am not prepared for your gaze. As you can see by my hands, I am covered in blood; my tunic is soiled. I must prepare for the ritual, so I don't insult the gods, please take the offerings. I will join you in the plaza for the dedication."

Anthony did a skillful job. If Rosalia wanted to she could have criticized his pronunciation of several words under different circumstances, but given the situation and the acoustics the lords could hardly have noticed.

Rosalia felt a tug on her arm and all of a sudden lightness; they had taken her brazier, and then Anthony's. The transfer had been made.

Lord Scab Scrapper answered," Pitan, don't be long. We need you for the ritual dedication and to interpret the sky vision. The hearts need to be still burning for a complete ritual."

The sky vision was the reading or interpretation of the smoke patterns that would indicate if the sacrifice was received successfully. Only a priest would be able to verify the god's acceptance. In this one matter, Pitan had more power than the lords. Too bad he couldn't be there for his moment of glory.

"I will my lords," Anthony replied.

And then their voice became distant. Rosalia could hear Lord Scab Scrapper saying that his brazier must contain the heart of the female because the smell was so sweet. It was ironic. He was right, his brazier contained the burning copal and Lord Jaundice held Pitan's. heart.

They pulled the door closed.

CHAPTER 17

They knew that they didn't have much time before the lords would return wondering what had happened to Pitan.

"What do we do? We can't run away since there is no where to run to."

"I think I know where the entrance is to Xibalba," Anthony said. He immediately corrected himself. "I mean the exit is."

"Where? Why haven't you shown it to me before? Why didn't we leave days ago?"

"Well, in a way I did show it to you. I only just realized what it is. You remember the tower and the walled structure?"

"Yes. You mean the one with the strange light?"

"I think that is a cave," he said.

"If it is a cave or exit, it's going the wrong direction…down." Rosalia was confused.

"I think it is an underwater cave, that, I mean it is the…"

"You mean like the underwater sites you were working on?"

"Exactly. We never fully explored the end of the cave site. I have no idea where the end of the cave would have led."

"You think that the cave was a real portal to Xibalba?"

"Yes, in one cave we found a paved road that ended with a column standing in front of a large pool of water. There were also temples close to the water and some actually under the water." The last cave we explored had a cenote shaped like an old Chianti bottle—a narrow neck leading to a wide chamber about 90 feet across and 120 feet deep. There were stalactites dripping from the ceiling, and the roots of trees were spread on the walls in delicate dark webbing. We know that Mayans would throw their sacrificed victims into the sacred cenotes like the one at Chichén Itzá. We found nine skeletons down at the bottom; I had always presumed that they had been thrown into the cenote, but now, I am convinced."

"You think those were victims sacrificed in Xibalba and thrown into the bottom of the cenote, rather from our world? Wow."

"Exactly. If that's the case, this could be our way out."

"But that was up in the Yucatan. I am not aware of any large-scale cenotes or underwater cave systems here in Chiapas."

"Maybe we have just discovered the first. Whatever, it would appear to be our only option. I will give you full discovery rights," Anthony said smiling.

They opened the door and to their relief no one was in sight. They heard someone coming, but before they could duck back into the temple, they saw the intruder to be their trusty canine scampering up the stairs. They began to hear a distant chanting; the Lords were beginning their ritual celebration, minus the chorus of attendants and accompanying music. It would appear that due to the lack of recent arrivals to Xibalba, they had harvested the population in order to satisfy the need for sacrificial offerings. They would be expecting Pitan to arrive to oversee the ceremony.

"I think we should run and not walk." Anthony could sense that the time was running out. The lords would return if the priest didn't show up soon. They both helped one another untie Pitan's arms from their own. With a dull thud his lifeless extremities fell to the floor. The dog immediately grabbed his right arm and ran off. Obviously, Pitan's limbs would provide an unexpected dog treat.

They began to run in the direction they had come in. This time it felt exhilarating. The procession of the lords and their impending doom seemed so distant even though they were still hostages of Xibalba. But now they, at least, had a plan. They rounded the intersection. To their right was the palace and what was now a series of loud chants and to their left was the walled enclosure, or what Anthony hoped was the cenote that would be the conduit for their escape.

The walls were imposing. Rosalia began to worry. "How are we possibly going to climb over? You don't have enough rope and I don't think that there is anything that I have seen in your backpack that will assist us.

"Don't worry. I think our answer is just around the corner."

They turned the corner, and Anthony pointed at the tower where they had been summoned by the attendant to follow him to the Temple. It was spectacular, identical to the tower at the Place at Palenque with the same 4 levels with stairs ascending through a series of corbelled vaults. They both were wondering if this was another sign that Pakal had been there. The light that was reflecting off of the upper floors would seem to validate Anthony's suspicion that the wall enclosed an outside portal. The shimmering effect of the light would suggest that it was being reflected through water. There was no guard as in the past. If this were truly an exit out of the underworld, the lords would have their secret heavily guarded. They began to climb the stairs. Like the twin tower at Palenque, the wear patterns were mainly on the inner edges of the stair surfaces indicating that the pedestrians over time had been gravitating to the center, possibly fearful of falling off of the tower. Rosalia was now leading the way. At about half way up the fourth floor, she let out a loud gasp.

"What is it? What is wrong?" asked Anthony.

"Nothing. I see the light and you were right. There is water."

"Our cenote."

"Exactly. This is our way out," she assured him.

They both got to the upper floor and stood and looked over the large enclosed well. The light was beautiful; it seemed to be radiating from an indirect source also validated Anthony's idea. There was a little bit of a problem. The distance from the tower seemed to be ten feet or more, easily more than either one of them would attempt to jump. Then they heard someone coming up the stairs. It was their mascot. This time his cute little face was partially hidden by the remains of Pitan's arm. His face was covered in blood, and he seemed extremely content. He dropped the bones at their feet. It almost seemed as though he wanted to play fetch with them.

They both began to giggle.

"Good boy," Rosalia patted him on his back.

"We don't have time for this," Anthony rushed. "We need to find a way to get to the wall."

Rosalia was the first to notice that short wall of the tower that faced the enclosure was made of wood and not limestone masonry like the rest. She began examining the wooden joints that held it together. The dog began to bark, something he had rarely done since their arrival. He went to the corner where she was standing and began scratching at the stone masonry that supported the tower and the wooden wall. He seemed focused and intent on the third stone block. To both their surprise the block fell to the floor. Revealing a wooden lever. The masonry was only a veneer. The dog stopped barking and sat. It was obvious he wanted to be rewarded. As disgusting as his bloody little head was, they both dropped to their knees and began petting him. He responded with the obligatory tail wag.

"What do you think the lever activates? A trap door? What?" asked Rosalia.

"I don't know if you noticed, but when we were walking toward the tower, there was a small ledge on the outside of the 4th floor wall," remembered Anthony.

She walked over and looked over the wall. Sure enough, there was a ledge approximately 3' wide running the length of the wall.

"It's a gang way," she announced with a sly smile.

"Well, in a sense it was more like a gang plank for the sacrificial victims, but for us it is a gangway of sorts."

Suddenly there was a loud rumbling. They looked toward the palace and could see the lords walking in their direction.

Anthony grabbed the lever. It wouldn't budge. Rosalia immediately grabbed the handle.

Counting down, "1-2-3," she jerked the handle towards her body.

At first nothing happened. Then the handle slowly pulled downward. Out of the corners of their eyes they could see the wall swing out ward towards the enclosure. The lords were now approaching the base of the tower.

Without hesitating Anthony began edging out onto the ledge, testing it. It was firm. He motioned for Rosalia to join him. Then the dog began to follow. Rosalie realized that the dog could not join them as they disembarked from the gangway. There was no way to get him through their underwater journey. The dog whimpered away to the far corner. It was as if they truly had betrayed an old friend. But this was no time for that kind of guilt.

The lords were rounding the second level stairwell when Anthony grabbed Rosalia's hand and said,"1-2-3."

They both jumped. The fall was long, and then they felt the shock of the cold water. Both swam to the surface, looking up they could see the lords. Outrages withdisbelief. They had never witnessed anyone return to the surface after they had gone into the well. Their victims had always had their hands and legs tied and their bodies weighted down to insure that the gods would accept the sacrifice. Lord Jaundice was the first to hurl his obsidian pointed spear, barely missing Rosalia. Then he aimed and threw two more, one lodging into Anthony's backpack. The Lords began to yell with excitement, knowing that they would have at least one victim. To their surprise Rosalia pulled the spear out and threw it at the wall, as Anthony and she began to swim to the opposite side of the cenote.

The Lords were in disbelief and angry. For a moment it looked as though Lord Jaundice was going to jump in after them, but his companions held him back. There was nothing they could do. Rosalia and Anthony were both relieved to see that they were not going to be pursued; however, they were still a long way from escaping Xibalaba.

How deep was the well? The depth was impossible to determine in these lighting conditions. Whatever the hole that the light source was emanating from could not be the direct exit. Obviously, the water would have drained out centuries ago. After appraising the situation, Anthony said, "I think we really only have one try at getting out. The longer we tread water, the more exhausted we will be. We need to take the deepest breaths we can and hold them and go down. If this is anything like the other water caves I have explored that are joined to cenotes, the hole leads to a tube and once we get to the level of the water in the well, it should turn into an airshaft escape tunnel.

"We will never know that we were wrong. We will just become one more offering."

She nodded and said,"1-2-3."

They both began swimming towards the light. It was disorienting at first swimming down to the light source, Anthony was the first to reach the opening and he waited briefly for Rosalia until she got to the mouth of the cave. He pushed her and immediately followed. They could see an even brighter light. Their ascent was slow, neither one of them had any oxygen left in their lungs to help them buoy to the surface. They finally got their breath, simultaneously they both kissed, something each of them had thought about and anticipated since they had entered Xibalba, not knowing if either one of them would experience intimate contact again.

The lava tube that had formed the air chamber was typical of others, with the characteristic ribbed texture that banded in neat horizontal formations around the walls. It was a perfect ladder. Anthony went first towards the surface opening that appeared to be approximately 20' high. Before ascending Anthony took out his rope and tied one end to his belt and Rosalia did the same to hers. She didn't question him since she knew he had much more experience with spelunking, a word that she loved to say more than doing.

Even though the bands provided a natural stairway, they were damp and slippery. Slowly they made their way up when Anthony pulled himself up to top and then was out of Rosalia's sight. She heard him scream something and couldn't make out what he said. She was sure that somehow the lords had made their way though a secret passageway and were there to escort them back to Xibalba. She felt the tug on her rope that confirmed her fears. They couldn't wait to get her. And then she saw Anthony's head peering over the edge smiling.

"W-what is it. What is wrong?"

"I have a big surprise for you," he answered.

"Please no more surprises."

Hesitating she asked, "Is it a good one?"

"The best."

She was almost at the top when Anthony lowered his hand and helped her over the edge. They were on the edge of what looked like another cenote, only this time she could see the light of the mouth of the cave and the silhouette of what looked like a replica of a Mayan Temple; in fact it looked like the Temple of Inscriptions.

Before she could say anything, Anthony said, "Welcome to my world."

She immediately knew what he meant; this was the cave he had described and explored right before she met him at Palenque.

"Isn't this amazing?"

Before he could say anything more, Rosalia's practical side kicked in.

"Amazing. It is impossible. It has to be another Xibalban illusion. The lords are trying to trick us. How can this be your cave? Anthony, think. Your cave is in the Yucatan 800 miles from Palenque, I know we were walking forever. Were you paying attention to your watch? I just thought mine was running very slowly, and then I would occasionally check yours for the same time and the same calendar date."

Anthony was still not following. Then he looked at his watch, something he hadn't done since he had low battery. Wasn't this what she meant?

"How many days have we been gone according to your watch?" she asked.

"Six," Anthony checked his watch again.

"Exactly, There is no way we could have gone that far."

"Maybe there was a magnetic field. I just know this is my cave. The only way we will know is to get out of here."

Rosalia still was a little hesitant, thinking that the lords would be waiting. Anthony was the first to swim across the well. Exhausted Rosalia slowly dog paddled across to the other side. She got out. Her eyes began to adjust to the light coming from the cave's opening. There was no mistaking sunlight and then she saw something else she hadn't seen for some time… the color green. It was brilliant. As they got to the cave's mouth they could smell the freshness of the air. The dull light and stagnate odor of Xibalba was only a memory.

"This is my cave, I can see the village of Tahtzibichen. I still have an apartment there. We are almost home," Anthony said excitedly.

"We can't tell anyone about this Anthony," Rosalia said still panting.

"No one would believe us anyway," Anthony smiled and hugged her.

EPILOGUE

It had been a year since Rosalia and Anthony had immerged from the biggest adventure of their lives. Rosalia was working as a post doc researcher at the Smithsonian in Washington, D.C. and Anthony was completing his book, *Underworld Cities of the Mayan*. It was ironic that he could use little of the knowledge he had gained from the Xibalba experience, since none of it could be verified. Rosalia and he agreed that if they discussed their experiences with anyone it would be the end of their careers. They would become a bigger laughing stock than Erich von Daniken and his book, *Chariots of the Gods,* when he claimed that aliens had built the pyramids.

Their experience had changed their lives in other ways. They were living together, occasionally talking about Xibalba. Both finally felt that they could move on knowing that adventure would always be part of their lives and an amazing bond in their relationship. They never realized how soon the underworld would become part of their world.

THE END